"Perhaps you could get a stick and draw a line down the beach on the boundary. I promise I won't cross it."

"But how much can I trust your promise?"

Alexa knew she'd regret letting her normally even temper get the better of her, but at this moment it exhilarated her. "Enjoy the rest of your stay in New Zealand." With a brisk little air she held out her hand.

Luka's long fingers closed around hers. As his mouth branded her skin Alexa crossed a hidden boundary into wild, unknown territory.

She yanked her hand back. White-faced, grabbing for composure, she said shakily, "Is that how you say goodbye in Dacia?"

"That's how we say I want you very much in Dacia," he drawled. "But you already knew that. And you want me, too. I hope you find it as irritating as I do."

She swallowed. "I'm going. Goodbye."

His laugh was low and unamused, totally cynical. "I think we'll see each other again."

"Not if I see you first," she shot back.

ROBYN DONALD has always lived in Northland in New Zealand, initially on her father's stud dairy farm at Warkworth, then in the Bay of Islands, an area of great natural beauty where she lives today with her husband and an ebullient and mostly Labrador dog. She resigned her teaching position when she found she enjoyed writing romances more, and now spends any time not writing in reading, gardening, traveling and writing letters to keep up with her two adult children and her friends.

Books by Robyn Donald

HARLEQUIN PRESENTS®
2246—THE DEVIL'S BARGAIN

Robyn Donald

THE PRINCE'S PLEASURE

By Royal Command

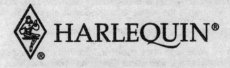

HARLEQUIN®

TORONTO • NEW YORK • LONDON
AMSTERDAM • PARIS • SYDNEY • HAMBURG
STOCKHOLM • ATHENS • TOKYO • MILAN • MADRID
PRAGUE • WARSAW • BUDAPEST • AUCKLAND

ISBN 0-373-12274-8

THE PRINCE'S PLEASURE

First North American Publication 2002.

Visit us at www.eHarlequin.com

Printed in U.S.A.

CHAPTER ONE

THE hotel events organiser burst into the drab staff cloakroom with all the drama of a star going nova, her frown easing dramatically when she saw the woman there.

'Alexa! Thank heavens!' she cried. 'I was afraid you weren't going to be able to make it. This wretched flu has struck down just about every waiter with security clearance.'

'Hi, Carole,' Alexa Mytton said cheerfully, smoothing sheer black pantyhose up her long legs. 'I didn't know I had security clearance.'

Carole looked a little self-conscious. 'With all the high-powered bankers in Auckland for this conference— not to mention the Prince of Dacia's security man, who is driving us crazy—head office insisted we run checks on everyone,' she said. 'You're as clean as a whistle, of course.'

Something in her voice alerted Alexa. 'Did you mention that I'm a photographer?'

A grimace distorted Carole's perfectly made-up face. 'No, because paranoia reigns! I could see I didn't have a hope of convincing the Prince's man that you're an up-and-coming studio photographer, not one of the dreaded paparazzi!'

Five years previously, when Carole had owned the top restaurant in the city, she'd hired Alexa as part-time help. A first-year university student, with no family and no money, Alexa had been grateful for the job, and still enjoyed helping her former boss in emergencies.

'Security men are paid to be paranoid,' she said cheerfully, straightening up to pull a long black skirt over her head. She patted the material over her slender hips and shrugged into a classical white shirt.

'He's not too bad, I suppose.' Carole surveyed Alexa with a professional eye. 'I thought you might have stopped taking casual work.'

'No, I'm still saving for that trip to Italy to research my grandfather.'

'Tell me when you're planning to go so I can take you off the roster.'

Alexa's long fingers flew as she buttoned up the shirt. Laughing, she said, 'It'll be another couple of months. But even if I had the tickets I'd have jumped at the chance to see the Grand Duke Luka of Dacia close up.' Opening her wide ice-grey eyes to their fullest extent, she batted long black lashes and simpered. 'He's not a regular visitor to unfashionable countries like New Zealand, so this might be my only chance to admire the gorgeous face that's sold so many millions of magazines and newspapers.'

Carole leaned forward, her voice dropping into a confidential purr. 'Mock all you like, but he's a seriously, seriously beautiful man.'

'Let's hope I can control my awe and fascination enough not to tip the crayfish patties over him.'

Oh, to be twenty-three again, Carole thought, before remembering what it had been like to ride that roller-coaster of emotions. But it would be great to *look* twenty-three again! Not that she'd ever come up to Alexa's standard. With her warm Mediterranean colouring of cream skin and copper hair the younger woman glowed like an exotic flower in the cramped, utilitarian confines of the room.

'*Not* patties,' Carole corrected briskly. 'They went out with the fifties. Did the Italian university have any information about your grandfather?'

Alexa shrugged. 'A big fat nothing so far.' Skillfully and swiftly she began to plait her thick hair into a neat roll at the back of her head. 'Either they won't give out information, or my Italian is so bad they didn't understand my letter!'

'That's a shame,' Carole said with brisk sympathy, glancing down at the clipboard she carried. She looked up to add, 'By the way, dishy though he certainly is, Luka of Dacia is no longer Grand Duke. Since his father died a year or so ago he's the hereditary Prince of Dacia, sole scion of the ancient and royal house of Bagaton.'

Alexa searched in her bag for a tube of lipgloss. 'What do I call him if he says something to me?'

'Your Royal Highness the first time, and then sir.' Carole sighed. 'It doesn't seem fair, does it? For a man to have it all—power, money and looks. Oh, and intelligence.'

Alexa laughed. 'Intelligence? Come off it, the man's a playboy.'

'He didn't get to be head of one of the top banks in the world without brains.'

'The fact that his royal daddy set the bank up might just have had something to do with that,' Alexa suggested drily, producing the tube from its hiding place in the bottom of her bag. 'If the gossip columns and royal-watchers of the world are right, the Prince simply hasn't got enough time to be a high-flying banker. He's too busy wining, dining and bedding fabulous women all over the globe.'

Carole grinned. 'Just wait till you see him. He's—well, he's overwhelming.'

'I haven't been able to open a magazine or newspaper for the past ten years without being overwhelmed by photographs of him. I agree—he's sinfully good-looking if you like them tall, dark and frivolous.'

'Frivolous he is not, and photographs don't do him justice. Whatever the definition of charisma, he's over-flowing with it. And trouble.' Abruptly sobering, Carole went on, 'Overseas photographers have already approached several of the staff with outrageous offers.'

'I knew I should have brought a camera—I could have hidden it down my front, James Bond style,' Alexa said, skimming her generous mouth with colour. 'One photograph of him carousing with bankers would probably finance my trip to Europe.'

'You're not big enough to hide anything much there. Neat, but not overblown, that's you. Have you got a camera with you?'

Alexa shook her head. 'Didn't seem tactful.'

'You're so right,' the older woman said, adding thoughtfully, 'The Prince of Dacia is not a man I'd like to cross.'

The hand wielding the lipstick suddenly still, Alexa met Carole's shrewd eyes in the mirror. 'A puffed-up playboy princeling, is he? Full of his own importance?'

'Far from it, according to those who've dealt with him. The staff say he's lovely.'

'But?' Alexa finished applying the gloss and snapped the case shut, scanning her reflection. She looked up and said quickly, 'Don't answer that—I'm sorry I asked. I know you have to be discreet.'

Carole said thoughtfully, 'He's the sort of man you notice, and it's not just the overwhelming combination of a handsome face, a great body and a height of about six foot four! It comes from inside him.'

Intrigued by the older woman's unusual gravity, Alexa turned her head. 'What does?'

'Charisma, I suppose. I saw him talking to the manager, being welcomed to the hotel—the sort of thing he's probably done thousands of times before. But there was no sign of boredom.'

Alexa's brows rose. 'They train royalty from childhood in that sort of PR. They probably have lessons in charm, and how to control the facial muscles!'

'I know, yet I'll bet my paua pearls he's no aristocratic figurehead. I got the impression that simmering beneath that very worldly surface there was a kind of fierce energy. He looks powerful.'

'So did King Kong. Now you've made him sound interesting.'

Carole shrugged. 'Unfortunately, not just to you. If someone starts asking questions about him, or for information about his movements, tell Security.'

Pulling a disgusted face, Alexa dropped the lipgloss into her bag. 'I will.'

'And thanks again for stepping into the breach.' Carole glanced at her watch. 'Help—I'd better go! If you get into trouble, smile—it's a killer, your smile.'

'It won't work if I ruin someone's designer outfit,' Alexa said pragmatically. 'I've been practising a demure, respectful expression all afternoon. Thank heavens a cocktail party's nowhere near as arduous as a silver service dinner.'

Carole shuddered. 'As of five minutes ago we've got a full muster of waiters for the banquet. Pray that it stays like that! Come on, I'll take you down. You might get a chance to use your Italian.' She opened the door to the corridor. 'Apparently Dacian has close similarities.'

Alexa had learned Italian at school and later, after her parents' death, at university, preparing for the day she'd go to Italy and find her grandfather's grave—perhaps even discover family there.

Of course an illegitimate granddaughter might not be welcome, but it would ease some inner loneliness just to know that she wasn't entirely on her own in the world.

During the turmoil of last-minute preparations, Alexa gave her respectful, self-effacing smile another couple of work-outs before she picked up a silver salver exquisitely decorated with tiny, tasty oyster savouries. Holding it steady, she set off into the room where the most powerful and influential people in the financial world, and their wives or mistresses—with a sprinkling of important politicians and local dignitaries—were meeting for drinks before dinner.

There she circulated slowly, careful not to let her interest in the women's clothes get in the way of her job.

She was covertly eyeing one trophy wife, clad in what appeared to be almost transparent scarlet clingwrap, when an autocratic female voice commanded from behind, 'Waitress, this way, please.'

Alexa's helpful, obliging smile slipped a fraction. There was always one snag.

Lovely, and superbly dressed, the snag was definitely not a trophy wife. She had a conscious air of power, Alexa decided as she eased her way through the crowd.

'Are those made with oysters?' the woman asked.

Alexa smiled, demure, self-effacing, and answered, 'Yes, they are,' as she proffered the salver.

Smiling up at the man beside her, the woman said in

an entirely different tone, 'Do try these, sir—they're a New Zealand speciality. We consider our Bluff oysters to be the finest in the world!'

'A big claim,' a deep, cool male voice responded with courteous confidence.

Alexa stole a glance through her lashes at an exquisitely tailored dinner suit that revealed wide shoulders, lean hips and long, strongly muscled legs.

Aha, she thought flippantly, the charismatic, much-photographed Prince Luka Bagaton of Dacia. And every bit as handsome as his photographs! The superbly chiselled features made an instant impact, as did a mouth that managed to combine beauty, strength and formidable self-discipline.

And then her eyes met his. Tawny-gold, the colour of frozen fire, they surveyed her with unsparing assessment.

Alexa stiffened as though she'd been measured, judged, and found wanting, and the salver in her hands quivered. Carole had chosen the right word for that formidable, potent aura of compelling maleness and authority. Prince Luka of Dacia was overwhelming—a devastating prince of darkness.

Heart juddering against her breastbone, Alexa concentrated on holding the salver steady while he took a savoury in a long, elegant hand.

'Thank you,' he said in that controlled voice with its fascinating slight accent.

Although Alexa had intended to step away without looking at him, her gaze flicked up to be captured by eyes gleaming with mockery. Yet a flare lightened their golden depths as the Prince of Dacia's bold warrior's face hardened into ruthlessness.

'Thank you, that's all we need.' The woman's voice, crisply territorial, slashed across Alexa's startled silence.

With a brief, meaningless smile she turned away, took
two steps and offered the salver to the next group.

Nobody had told her that charisma burned, she
thought once she drew breath again. Ridiculously, she
felt as though the Prince's brutally emphatic energy had
reached out and claimed her, branding her with a mark
of possession that scarred her all the way to her soul.

Striving desperately to recall her sense of humour, she
ordered herself not to be so idiotic. He'd looked at her;
she'd looked at him. And, being a strongly visual person,
she'd overreacted to the most gorgeous man she'd ever
seen!

Shaken, still tautly aware of the Prince in the middle
of the room, she avoided his area and kept her gaze well
away until everyone obeyed some unspoken signal and
trooped into the banqueting hall.

Much later, when her shift was over and she was
heading for the staff cloakroom, Carole appeared, looking slightly less harried. 'The banquet went off really
well—so far, so good,' she said on a quick, relieved
note. 'What did you think of the Prince?'

'Grand Duke suited him better—he's entirely too
grand,' Alexa said, aiming for her usual blithe tone and
just missing. 'Who's his minder?'

'The stunning blonde? Sandra Beauchamp, the under-
secretary for something or other. Apparently she's an old
flame.'

Repressing a stark stab of primitive emotion she
would not dignify with the name of envy, Alexa
drawled, 'Old? She wouldn't like to hear that.'

Carole gave her a sharp woman-to-woman grin.
'Warned you off, did she? I don't blame her—she'd be
mad not to try for another chance with him. So, what
did you think of him?'

Alexa hoped an ironic smile hid her erratic emotions. 'He's a fabulous man, like something out of a fairy story—one of the dark and dangerous ones.'

'He gave a fantastic after-dinner speech—funny, moving, intelligent and short!'

'I hope he paid the writer lots.'

'Methinks I detect a note of cynicism,' Carole said as they turned towards the service lift. 'Don't you approve of the monarchy?'

How could she say that Prince Luka had made such an impact on her she couldn't think straight? It sounded foolishly impetuous, like falling in love at first sight.

Alexa shrugged. 'As an institution I think it's probably on its way out, but our lot have done pretty well by us, so who am I to tell the Dacians how to run their country? If they like their Prince, that's fine. And I gather he's doing great things for them with his bank.'

Pressing the button to call the lift, Carole said in an awed voice, 'The bank uses the Dacian crown jewels as security.'

Suddenly tired, Alexa covered a yawn. 'Crown jewels?' she said vaguely. 'Oh, yes, I remember—don't they have fabulous emeralds?'

'And the rest! Literally worth a prince's ransom.' The lift slid to a halt in front of them, doors opening. 'Have you got your car?' Carole asked, jabbing the button to keep the doors apart.

Alexa shook her head. 'It's in dry dock. Something to do with the radiator, I think. Whatever, it made funny noises.'

'Then take a taxi—and keep the receipt because you'll be reimbursed.'

'I'll drop it off or post it to you. Goodnight.'

After the lift had whirred Carole upwards Alexa took

the next one down to the ground floor, but one glance
at the foyer changed her mind about trying to get a taxi
there.

People were pouring out, taxis leaving as soon as
they'd arrived, doormen moving fast to clear the crowd.
Not to worry—the nearest taxi rank was only a couple
of hundred yards away, just around the corner of a well-
lit street. And as the hotel car park opened onto the same
street there'd be enough passing traffic to make it perfectly safe.

Slinging her bag over her shoulder, Alexa set off,
shivering slightly because it had rained while she'd been
offering delicious food to the rich and powerful.

Down in the basement car park, in the restricted area,
Luka of Dacia stood beside the anonymous car his agent
had hired and listened courteously to his head of security.

'At least let me follow you in another car,' Dion said
urgently. 'I don't like anything about this—why do they
want you to go alone to meet them?'

Luka said calmly, 'These men have been fighting a
desperate war for the past twenty years—a war that's
turned brother against brother, father against son. I don't
imagine they trust anyone any more.' He understood
their behaviour. His life had been built on a lack of trust.

'That's no reason to put yourself in their power,' Dion
expostulated angrily. 'Luka, I beg of you, think again!
Your father would never have permitted you to take such
a risk.'

'My father judged risks differently from you.'

Dion said in exasperation, 'Your father would have
risked everything for Dacia. This is not for Dacia—these
people are nothing to you—their Pacific island is as far

from Dacia as any place can be. Let them fight their
futile war until they're all dead!'

Luka's brows rose but his voice was crisp and abrupt
as he said, 'Somehow I don't think it's quite as simple
as that. Apart from my obvious neutrality, they must
have a reason to choose me as an intermediary between
them and their opponents.'

'What possible reason can they have?'

'That's what I plan to find out. These people aren't
rebels—they are the elected government of Sant'Rosa.
So they're not going to kill or kidnap me. And apart
from the humanitarian aspects I have also to consider
that although their country may be in ruins now it has
the largest copper mine in the Asian Pacific region, not
to mention other extremely valuable minerals, and the
possibility of a flourishing tourist industry. Good pick-
ings for the bank.'

Dion, who knew perfectly well that it was the humanitarian aspects that had persuaded his Prince, said
angrily, 'Why ask for this secret meeting late at night
and alone?'

'Possibly because they don't want to lose face. If tonight leads to further discussions between the two fac-
tions on Sant'Rosa, and if I can persuade them to accept
some sort of protocol for peace, the Bank of Dacia can
help them rebuild their economy. By ensuring their pros-
perity, I can help promote ours.' He paused, then added
coolly, 'My father would have thought any—every—
sacrifice worth that.'

Dion's frown deepened at the complete determination
in his Prince's voice. 'Let me come with you,' he said,
knowing it was hopeless. 'No one will know I'm there.'

'I will know,' Luka said inflexibly. 'I gave them my
word I'd go alone, and I intend to keep it.' He looked

down at the man he called friend and demanded, 'Give me your word you won't do anything to jeopardise this meeting.'

Dion met the Prince's hard eyes with something like anguish. 'You have it,' he said stiffly, and stood back, holding the door open to let his ruler into the car.

Luka slid behind the wheel, his face sombre as he turned the key and heard the engine purr into life. Although he was early for the meeting, he was also a stranger to Auckland, so in spite of memorising the route he'd probably make enough wrong turnings to use up the extra hour.

Putting the car into gear, he eased it out of the parking bay and through the car park, slid his card into the slot and waited for the grille to roll back.

A security man posted there gave him a keen look and a respectful nod—another instance of the meticulous attention to detail by the conference planners.

The wet street appeared deserted, but his eyes narrowed when he saw a woman striding towards the corner; adrenalin pumped through him as he noticed the two men coming up behind her, leashed violence smoking around them like an aura. They were taking care not to make a noise—hunters with prey in their sights.

Luka's hand thudded onto the horn and he stamped on the accelerator. The stalked woman jumped and whirled, mouth opening in a scream he could hear even over the squealing tyres and revving engine. By the time he'd driven across the footpath between her and the men she'd backed into the wall, hands in front of her in a classic posture of self-defence.

Trained? No, but ready to defend herself, Luka guessed with approval, himself expert in a lethal martial

art. He leapt out of the car, but the two men were already
sprinting across the street.

Luka ignored them. 'Are you all right?' he demanded
harshly.

The street lamp revealed a face he recognised, a face
that had lodged like a burr in his mind since she'd offered him a savoury before dinner. A highly appropriate
offering, he'd thought then—oysters for sexual stamina.
He'd looked into eyes, like a blast of winter set between
black lashes and brows, and wanted her with a violence
that startled and irritated him.

'I'm fine, thanks to you,' she said, the words coming
clumsily.

Although she was pale her wide, soft mouth was held
under tight discipline. Unwillingly Luka admired her
self-control even while some part of him wondered what
she'd look like when she lost it.

Wild; those fantastic ice-grey eyes half hidden by
heavy eyelids, her hair tossed and tumbled like skeins
of copper silk... The flush of passion would turn her
skin to peaches and cream, and her mouth would soften
into a sensuous welcome.

To take his mind off that purely male speculation—
and the stir it created in his body—he suggested quietly,
'You can drop your hands now. You're quite safe.'

They fell to her sides. She managed a rapid, set smile
and said, 'Thank you.'

'For what?'

Her teeth bit into her bottom lip for a moment before
she answered, 'For getting involved.'

'Why wouldn't I?'

'Some people don't,' she said, dragging a sharp breath
into her lungs.

Luka wrenched his gaze from the extremely interesting lift and fall of her breasts. In a voice he realised was too harsh, he demanded, 'Who are you, and just what are you doing in a back street at this time of night?'

'I'm Alexa Mytton,' she answered, stiffening as her chin came up, 'and I'm going to the taxi rank around the corner.'

'Why not ask one of the doormen to get you a cab?'

So he'd recognised her. Something warm and satisfied, a kind of purr of femininity, smoothed over Alexa. Afraid she'd fall apart if she relaxed, she straightened her shoulders and said quickly, 'I'm not a guest at the hotel. Thanks very much for being so quick to respond. I'll—I'll go now and get a taxi.'

'I'll walk there with you,' he said with a crisp purpose that warned her he wasn't going to leave her there alone.

Clamping down on a shiver, the aftermath of the terror that had surged through her, she said feebly, 'You can't leave your car blocking the way.'

'Then can I offer you a lift to the rank? You are really in no fit state to walk there by yourself.' A hint of impatience threaded his decisive voice.

Alexa knew she should say no and head briskly off. She glanced up into a face carved in granite, and then looked away, her stomach knotting; although definitely a dangerous man, there was no criminal menace about him. The peril radiating from him was the simple, sensual danger a potent male represented to a woman's composure.

'Thank you,' she said tightly, repressing another shiver.

With courteous speed the Prince put her into the front seat beside him and drove around the corner.

And of course the taxi rank was empty—as was the

street, apart from one man lurching from lamppost to lamppost. Alexa stifled a little hiss of dismay.

'If you'll trust me with your address I'll take you home,' the man beside her said with an aloofness that should have reassured her as he pulled into the empty space in the taxi rank, clearly not at all concerned by the prospect of any cruising cab-driver's outrage.

'Thank you, but you don't need to do that,' she told him swiftly. 'Perhaps you could take me to the nearest police station—if it's not too much trouble,' she added swiftly when he hesitated.

'Of course,' he said remotely, and put the car into gear again. When she'd given him instructions he said evenly, 'Promise me that you won't again walk by yourself at night in the inner city.'

'I don't make a habit of it. I was just in the wrong place at the wrong time,' she defended herself. 'I suppose they thought it would be easy enough to grab my bag and get away before anyone arrived.'

'Perhaps. And perhaps they didn't want money.'

'What else would they have wanted?' she asked, then flushed at his derisive glance. A slow cold shudder tightened her skin. She'd only had one glimpse of their faces before they'd turned and sprinted across the street, but they were imprinted on her mind. 'They can't possibly have thought they could get away with...assaulting me on a public street when traffic and pedestrians could arrive—'

'You forget the car,' he broke in. 'And surely your mother told you that beautiful women are always prey.'

'What car?' His words chilled her, yet she tingled because he'd called her beautiful.

The swift blade of the Prince's glance skimmed her

profile. 'They'd parked down that little alley over the street. Didn't you hear them drive off?'

'No.' Because her whole attention had been focused on him. Fear cramped her stomach as she realised how close she'd been to disaster. Alexa muttered through teeth she had to clench, 'It was just bad luck—'

'And foolishness,' he said with a bite in his tone, startling her by pulling into the kerb and shouldering free of his jacket.

Before she had time to say more than, 'What on—?' he tossed the garment at her. It landed on her lap, warm and as superbly cut as the dinner jacket he'd been wearing in the hotel.

'Wrap that around you,' he commanded, when she stared mutely at him. 'You're shocked and cold.'

Startled and dismayed, she pushed at the garment. 'I'm all right—'

'You're shivering,' he pointed out. When she didn't move—couldn't move—he commanded, 'Lean forward.'

Alexa reacted to the crack of authority in his words with automatic obedience. He dropped the garment around her shoulders, pulling it down to cover her arms.

As the cloth enfolded her sensation splintered in the pit of her stomach. Still warm from his body, the jacket sparked a violent, primal tug of awareness deep inside her, an awareness made keener, more intense by the faint, clean scent that had to be his—scent only a lover would recognise.

'All right?' he asked, frowning. He dropped his hands over hers, clasping them as he said more gently, 'You've had a very nasty experience, but it's over now. You're safe.'

'Thanks to you,' she muttered. Safe? When every cell in her body was drumming with a wild, strange need?

He said something in a language that sounded like Italian before freeing her and turning away to set the car in motion. As it pulled away from the taxi rank he asked in English, 'I have forgotten where we turn next.'

Still shaking inside, she gave him directions. Had he really said something like 'dangerously beautiful' in what must be his mother tongue?

Of course not. She tried to straighten her trembling mouth. In spite of a superficial resemblance, the Dacian language was not Italian.

But he found her attractive.

So what? Being rescued from what might have been an exceedingly nasty situation was no excuse for behaving like a halfwit. Prince Luka Bagaton of Dacia might possess courage and some kindness, he might even think she was beautiful, but he was way out of her reach—and she wasn't reaching! A quick fling with a visiting prince was not her style.

Alexa stiffened her spine and her shoulders. When the car stopped outside the police station she groped for the door handle and said in her most formal voice, 'Thank you very much for your help. I hope you enjoy the rest of your stay in New Zealand.'

After a quick glance at his watch, he said, 'I'll come in with you.'

Alexa objected. 'You don't need to become tangled up in this. You were on your way somewhere...'

To Sandra Beauchamp's bed, perhaps?

Without looking at her he said, 'I saw them too. I may be able to help identify them.'

'I…' She hesitated, then blurted, 'You don't want to get involved.'

'You're right,' he said, courteously inflexible, 'but it is my duty.'

CHAPTER TWO

HALF an hour later, after separate interviews, the sergeant complimented them both. 'I wish all our witnesses were as observant as you two! With such good descriptions we should nail them before they do any damage.' She looked at Alexa and said, 'We'll contact you if we need to.'

Alexa nodded. In the small room where she'd made her statement and drawn a sketch of both assailants she'd been given tea and some bracing, professional sympathy. It had helped, but her insides still felt as though someone had taken to them with a drill, and weak, irritating tears kept stinging her eyes.

Luka's firm hand on her elbow ushered her out to his car. 'You'll have to direct me to your address,' he said after a searching glance.

In a monotone Alexa guided him to her small flat in one of the inner city suburbs. He drove skilfully and well, although a couple of times she had to fill him in on New Zealand road rules.

Once they'd drawn up outside what had used to be a Victorian merchant's house, now converted to flats, she said sincerely, 'Thank you very much for everything you've done.'

The words stumbled to silence when he looked at her with cool, dispassionate irony, his angular features clamped into an expression of aloof withdrawal. Tension sparked through her, lifting the hair on her skin. Delayed shock, she thought protectively.

Swallowing, she continued with prickly determination, 'I don't like to think of what might have happened if you hadn't come along.'

'Don't think of it. Your scream would have brought someone running. I did nothing,' he said negligently and got out, swinging around the front of the car to open the door for her. 'But promise me one thing.'

Clinging to the door, she braced herself. He was too close, but even as the thought formed he stepped back and she pulled herself upright on quivering legs.

'What?' she asked, her throat tightening around the words so that they emerged spiky with caution.

His smile was a flash of white in the darkness—sexy, knowledgeable and implacable. 'That from now on you will call the doorman when you leave the hotel.'

'From tomorrow I'll be driving my own car, but I promise I won't go walking alone at night,' she responded quickly, groping in her bag for her keys. In her turn she smiled at him. Keep it impersonal, she warned herself, angry because she was so acutely conscious of him, tall and lethally masculine, his dark energy feeding some kind of hunger in her. 'And I don't work at the hotel,' she added.

His eyes narrowed. 'I saw you—'

'Handing out snacks,' she agreed. 'I'm on the emergency roster and I was called in tonight because flu is laying the staff low.' It seemed days ago now, as though the telephone call had summoned a different woman.

For someone who wanted to keep things on an impersonal level, she was failing miserably. Get out of here, she told herself silently. Now!

Walking carefully past him, she went up the steps to the front door, unlocked it and turned, to flinch back with dilating eyes at the tall, dominant silhouette that blocked out most of the light.

'I'm sorry,' he said harshly, hands closing around her upper arms. Warm, strong, unthreatening, they gave her support and steadiness. Frowning, he said, 'You're too pale. You've had a shock, and you should have someone to make sure you're all right.' His arms closed around her, pulling her into the hard warmth of his body.

In spite of the warnings hammering her brain, Alexa let herself lean on him, accepting the male comfort he offered with a purely female gratitude.

'You were brave,' he said on an unexpected note of gentleness. 'I saw you gauge your options and decide that screaming and fighting back offered the best chance. Quick thinking, and a refusal to accept being a victim. Do you know how to defend yourself?'

'No. I've always thought I should do s-something about it, but I've never s-seemed to have the time.' She stopped her stammered explanation to drag in a quick, shallow breath. It was dangerously sweet to be cosseted. Forcing a brisk note into her voice, she pulled away, both relieved and disappointed when he released her instantly. 'I'm sorry I interrupted your evening.'

He frowned, the dim light emphasising his brutally handsome features. 'It was nothing. Can I ring someone for you?'

'It's really not necessary—I'm a bit shaky, but a good night's sleep will fix that.' Alexa suddenly remembered his coat, still keeping her warm. 'Oh, your jacket!' She set her bag down on the balustrade and struggled to get out of it, hauling at the material so recklessly that her shirt lifted free of her waistband.

The Prince's hands skimmed the silken skin on either side of her waist, then jerked back as though the touch burned him. Alexa's breath froze in her throat. She stared up into eyes that glittered in the light of the street lamps, into a face as hard and tough as a bronze mask.

For the space of several heartbeats neither moved until Alexa regained her wits enough to leap back and hand over the jacket. Both were careful not to let their fingers touch.

'There,' she said in a strained, hoarse voice. 'And *don't* say it was nothing.'

His mouth compressed. In a voice that could have splintered stone, he said, 'I don't lie. Go inside.'

Taut with a forbidden excitement, Alexa opened the door and escaped into the hall. 'Goodbye.'

His dark head inclined. 'Goodbye, Alexa Mytton.'

Incredulous, she thought she heard an echo of aloneness that mirrored her own. She looked up sharply, but his hard face revealed nothing except self-contained assurance. Heart hammering, Alexa pushed the door closed with an abrupt thud.

She listened until the sound of the car engine was lost in the noise of other vehicles, and then walked along to her flat, thinking that of all the idiotic things to suspect in Prince Luka loneliness was probably the most unlikely.

Yet he was far from the playboy prince she'd imagined, a handsome surface-skimmer, all machismo and conceit. He'd changed from a warrior, quick-thinking, formidable and exceedingly dangerous, to a man who offered aloof kindness and an inherent protectiveness that still surprised her.

Luka Bagaton was a complex, deeply interesting man. 'S-sexy, too,' she said aloud.

In the chilly security of her own flat she glanced at her reflection in the mirror, wincing at the feverish gleam

in her pale eyes and the hectic flush along her cheekbones.

She had every right to feel jumpy and restless, but she
wasn't going to be able to sleep like this. Still trembling
inside, she made herself a cup of milky chocolate, took
it across to her computer and sat down to log on, searching for Luka Bagaton on the internet.

An hour later she switched off the computer and got
up, stretching muscles that had locked as she'd read
about Prince Luka of Dacia.

'No wonder he's so self-contained,' she said, picking
up the empty mug of chocolate.

At eighteen his father had succeeded to a princedom
on the verge of being invaded by a country across the
narrow strait separating the island of Dacia from Europe.
Then, amazingly—and probably desperately—he'd married the only child of the dictator who'd threatened his
country. His ploy had worked—Dacia had kept a limited
independence. A year later the only child of the union
had been born.

'I hope they fell in love,' Alexa said, yawning. 'Otherwise it would have been hell for them both.'

Ten minutes before she had to leave for work the next
morning, Alexa's bell pealed. Her brows drew together
as she pushed proof sheets into an envelope and went
out to answer the chiming summons.

She opened the door to a man carrying a huge bunch
of Peruvian lilies, delicately formed and fragile in shades
of copper.

'Miss Alexa Mytton?' the messenger asked. At her
nod he held them out.

Alexa automatically took the lovely things, looking
down at the envelope with her name written across it in

bold, very definite letters. Her heart jolted as she said, 'Thank you.'

Back in her flat she arranged them in a glass vase in front of the window, admiring the way the autumn sunlight glowed through the silky, almost translucent petals. Had he chosen them to match her hair?

Only then, overcoming a kind of superstitious reluctance, she opened the envelope. *I hope you are feeling much better this morning,* he'd written, signing it with an arrogant 'L'.

A swift shimmer of excitement took her by surprise. They were lovely, she thought, touching one of the lilies with a gentle forefinger.

Oh, all right, he'd probably said to someone, Send some flowers to this address, please, and forgotten about it immediately, but it was thoughtful of him. She swung around and caught up her camera. If only she could catch that silken transparency...

Glancing at her watch, she regretfully put the camera down. It would have to wait.

Alexa stamped into the flat late that afternoon, still tense after a hideous session with an actress who'd insisted on being photographed with her pair of psychopathic Dobermanns, laughing brightly every time they made a determined attempt to eat Alexa's equipment.

The Peruvian lilies gleamed like copper tulle when she turned on the light, and her strained irritation mutated into a sweet, futile anticipation.

Carole had rung to say she had a full roster, so Alexa knew she wouldn't see Prince Luka again, but she'd always remember his kindness and his flowers. She'd written a note to thank him for them, and would drop it off at the hotel in a few minutes.

The front doorbell jangled through the room. 'Oh, great!' she said, slinging her bag onto a chair. Perhaps it was a friend who'd called in for coffee.

But the man who waited there was no friend, although he looked vaguely familiar.

Before she had time to place him he spoke in an accent that told her what that familiarity was. 'Miss Mytton?'

Her heart picked up speed. 'I'm Alexa Mytton.'

'The Prince wishes to see you,' he told her impassively, although the dark eyes that lingered on her face were shrewd and perceptive. 'I'm sorry it's such short notice, but if you could come with me...'

When she hesitated he frowned and said, 'I am sorry.' He drew out a card and presented it with some ceremony.

He was Dion, followed by a long Dacian name. Alexa turned the card over, her eyes scanning the writing on the back—Prince Luka's writing.

Please accompany Dion, it said, the brief note followed by that same 'L'.

She was probably being paranoid after last night, but she wasn't getting into a car with a total stranger. 'I'm going past the hotel in ten minutes,' Alexa said. 'I'll call in on my way.'

He looked taken aback, but said politely, 'Yes, of course. I will meet you at the elevators on the third floor.'

Secretly, shamefully glad she was wearing a sleek trousersuit in her favourite bronze, with a silk mesh tank top under the blazer-cut jacket, Alexa closed the door on him and scurried back into the flat to renew her lipstick, before scooping up her car keys.

Why did Prince Luka want to see her? Expectant, yet

strangely apprehensive, she parked in the visitors' car
park and took the lift into the hotel.

Sure enough, Dion with the mile-long name was waiting. Although he greeted her cordially enough she
sensed his reservation as he opened another elevator with
a key and ushered her inside. Kites jostling in her stomach, she stared at the wall until the lift stopped at the
penthouse, where a security guard opened the door and
ushered them both into a foyer.

'In here, madam,' her guide said, opening another
door for her.

He stood back as Alexa walked through. Stopping
when the door closed behind her, she ignored the huge,
opulently furnished room to fix her eyes on the man who
turned from contemplation of a crimson sunset to look
at her with dangerous metallic eyes.

From somewhere Alexa remembered that when confronted by royalty you waited until you were spoken to.
So, although she had to bite back the words that trem-
bled on her tongue as he surveyed her with comprehen-
sive and intimidating thoroughness, she stood silently.

But her eyes sparkled at his unsparing scrutiny, and
her mouth tightened as she jutted her chin at him.

'Have you seen today's newspaper?' he asked in a
deep, cold voice.

Frowning, she abandoned any attempt at formality and
protocol. 'No. Why?'

He gestured at one spread out on a coffee table. 'Perhaps you should read it now. In the last section, page
three.'

After a baffled glance she walked across to the table
and picked up the paper. The conference had made the
front page, but the part he referred to was a lifestyle
pullout. And there, in the gossip column, someone had

ringed an item with a slashing black pen—the same pen that had written the letter 'L' on the paper accompanying her flowers.

Incredulously Alexa read the item.

The Prince of Dacia, heaven's gift to romantic roy-alists now that the Prince of Illyria is married, is clearly a connoisseur of more in New Zealand than our scenery and wine. Last night, a small but dedi-cated bird told me, he was seen driving one of Auckland's busiest young photographers home after the opening banquet of the banking conference. And she was wearing his jacket. What, we wonder, can this mean?

With scornful precision he asked, 'Did you leak this?'

Alexa's head jerked upwards. Bitterly—foolishly—hurt, she transfixed him with a furious glare. 'Of course I didn't!'

'Then how did it get into the newspaper?'

She didn't know what intimidated her more—his an-ger, frozen and harsh as a blizzard at the South Pole, or his flinty control.

'I don't know,' she told him, clinging to her compo-sure. 'Someone saw us at the police station, I'd imagine. Fortunately she hasn't linked you with any specific per-son.'

'Perhaps your name will be in the next sly little mor-sel,' he said with a cutting edge to his voice.

Her head jerked around and she met the full shock of his gaze. Dry-mouthed, she asked, 'Why should there be a next one?'

'Because whoever fed this to the columnist will make sure of it.'

'Look,' she said, trying to be reasonable, 'it's irritating and naff, but it isn't the end of the world. People will forget it.'

'I won't forget it,' he said, watching with hooded eyes the way the light smouldered across her hair, loose now around her face. With silky precision he said, 'I don't like being used, Ms Mytton.'

In the face of his scornful arrogance she felt hot and foolish and furious. Covering a stab of pain with seething denial, she asked indignantly, 'Why would I want to *use* you?'

'Usually it's for money,' he returned caustically, killing Alexa's jab of sympathy by adding, 'But often for notoriety—and I imagine that a link to me, however tenuous, would help you advance in your profession. I hope you took no photographs of me last night.'

Pale eyes glittering, Alexa almost ground her teeth. Her quip to Carole about hiding a camera came back to taunt her, bringing colour to her skin—which he noticed. 'Not a single one,' she retorted crisply. 'And I don't leak titbits to the press. This rubbish—' she gestured contemptuously at the newspaper '—is your area, not mine. And it's totally without any foundation.'

'Do you really believe that?' He crossed the room in two strides, stopping her instinctive retreat by grasping her shoulders.

The previous night Alexa had noticed the strength and support of his hands; now, knocked off-balance by hurt and anger, she felt nothing but the promise of their power.

'I wish I could believe that there is no foundation for the sly innuendo in that rubbish,' he said, mockery gleaming in the frozen fire of his eyes, 'but I am a realist above all else.'

And he bent his head and kissed her.

Afterwards Alexa tried hard to convince herself that it was the sheer unexpectedness that kept her locked un-protesting in his embrace.

But she lied. The second she'd seen Luka she'd been acutely, forcefully aware of him—and in spite of his steely control, she'd recognised a like response. Each time their eyes had met they'd exchanged hidden mes-sages that bypassed logic to kick-start a flagrant hunger.

Fed by clamouring instincts, that secret communica-tion—primitive and involuntary—had grown in quantum leaps, burning away common sense and caution.

Without realising it, she'd been waiting for this mo-ment, all that was female in her knowing it would come. In mute surrender, she relaxed against his taut body.

At the first touch of his mouth something buried inside Alexa split and broke, as though she'd emerged from a chrysalis.

And then, after a kiss as short, brutal and impersonal as a slap, Luka lifted his head to survey her with chilling detachment, the hunger that prowled his eyes disappear-ing behind their opaque, enamelled surface.

It took every ounce of self-command she could sum-mon to ask sweetly, 'Had enough?' letting contempt sharpen each word.

With a bleak, twisted smile he said harshly, 'Unfor-tunately, no.'

This time the kiss was neither brief nor brutal. He kissed her with fire and purposefulness, as though he'd longed for her down the years, as though they were lov-ers who had only this kiss to exchange before bitter fate tore them apart for ever.

Alexa struggled to remain passive, but a terrifyingly raw, untamed force sprang up to meet his open hunger, and—to the shocked astonishment of the last rational part of her mind—match it. Flames rocketed through her, eating away everything but the sheer physical magic of the Prince's flavour and subtle scent, and the heat and power of his warrior's body against hers.

It was the increasing hardness of that body rather than the sharp knock on the door that broke into her sensual enslavement. In some dim recess of her brain she remembered that this man might have spent the night with another woman.

When she pushed against his chest he lifted his head and released her, stepping back. Alexa forced her lashes up and looked into eyes as polished and impersonal as the gold they resembled. Oh, he wanted her—he couldn't hide that—but with nothing more complex than simple lust.

It shouldn't have hurt.

Yet it was pain as much as fury that drove her to ask, 'And what did that prove, except that you're stronger than I am?'

Caustic amusement gleamed in his gaze, curved the mouth that now knew hers intimately. 'It proved that you want me as much as I do you,' he returned on a note of courtesy that lacerated her composure.

'That means nothing,' she retorted, trying to convince herself. Beneath the surface control, she realised, he was blackly furious.

'An admirably liberated view,' he said, not hiding the flick of contempt in his tone.

The skin over her high cheekbones heated and she forgot tact and discretion and plain common sense to flare, 'Perhaps, but *I'm* not so liberated that I sleep with every good-looking man who wants a bit of publicity.'

'No,' he said lethally, 'you merely pander to the avid eagerness of people who want to read that sort of trash.'

Hot with chagrin at her humiliating rudeness, she said between her teeth, 'I shouldn't have said that. I'm sorry. But, for the last time, I did *not* notify the newspaper.'

He surveyed her with aggression bordering on menace. 'If news of those kisses makes it into the media I'll know how much your word is worth.'

'As much as yours,' she said tersely. 'I'd hate to be as mistrustful as you are.'

'I imbibed it with my mother's milk,' he said, adding with cold distaste, 'Literally.'

Shocked by the stark authenticity in his words, she muttered, 'There's someone at the door.'

'They'll wait.'

Possibly his staff were accustomed to waiting for him to finish with the woman of the moment!

Alexa turned away, paradoxically feeling safer now they were back in adversarial mode. 'They won't have to. I'm going.'

'Perhaps you should comb your hair,' he suggested in a voice that was a maddening mix of amusement and mockery. 'You look—tumbled.'

Glaring at him, Alexa shook her hair back from her face, but the heavy copper tresses clung to her hot cheeks and temples. She pushed it back with her fingers, but when his dark gaze lingered on her shaking hands she gave up. With a crisp 'Goodbye' she walked abruptly towards the door.

Halfway there, she stopped. 'Thank you for the flowers.'

'Don't throw them into the garbage just because I sent them.' He sounded more than a little bored.

'It isn't their fault they came from you.' She couldn't

resist adding, 'Although I'll bet you ordered a minion to send them!'

'Alas, the days of minions are long past,' he said, deadpan, adding, 'Have you got your car back yet?'

'Yes, thank you.' Torn by a debilitating mixture of anger and resentment and desolation, she swept out past the man who waited on the other side of the door.

Luka's eyes met Dion's and he jerked his head. Obeying the unspoken order, Dion closed the door. He'd accompany her down to her car.

Alone once more, Luka turned away and walked across to the window, to stare at the elaborate terraced garden and pool outside.

Shortly after his seventh birthday he'd screwed his courage to the sticking point and dived through a waterfall to the pool behind it. He'd felt the way he did now—as though the gleaming darkness was a gateway into some other dimension, a place of perilous beauty where he risked the slow dissolution of his innermost self.

Every muscle clenched while he fought to leash an unwanted onslaught of desire. He understood the primitive strength of his own needs and instincts, and over the years he'd caged them in a prison of will-power and discretion.

Yet Alexa Mytton's smile and the glittering promise in those pale, crystalline eyes had pushed him over the knife-edge of control.

He shouldn't have kissed her, and once he'd done it he certainly shouldn't have surrendered to that overmastering need to find out whether she tasted as good the second time as she did the first.

He tried to resurrect his anger, but primal impulses

still raced recklessly through his cells. He had work to do.

He was leafing rapidly through papers when another knock at the door signalled Dion's return. When the other man was inside Luka asked, 'Did you see her to her car?'

Dion said abruptly, 'Yes. Luka, the last sighting of Guy was a week ago, when he boarded a ship loaded with medical supplies for Sant'Rosa. I've checked, but no one seems to know where it went or what happened to it.'

Luka swore—low, virulent oaths that startled his companion.

When he stopped Dion drew in a sharp breath and said, 'You'd better tell me what this is all about.'

'Guy is a hostage,' Luka said, only a thread of steel in the deep voice betraying his emotions.

Last night's meeting had begun in an atmosphere that had reeked with suspicion, but he had thought he'd managed to convince the men from Sant'Rosa that he was an entirely neutral emissary. They had discussed the sort of peace they envisaged.

And then they'd produced their trump card in the form of his cousin.

'In Sant'Rosa? We can spring him,' Dion said instantly.

'Without alerting the government?' Luka shook his head. 'He's safe enough for the present. They really want an end to this war, and they're convinced the rebels want it too. However, they don't trust anyone—not even anyone from the other side of the world.' His voice hardened into iron. 'When Guy appeared they recognised him from the gossip columns and realised they had the perfect way to stop me from double-crossing them. According to the Prime Minister, he is quite safe.'

'And you believe him?'

'That far, I believe him,' Luka said deliberately. 'And I believe that if any word of this peace initiative gets out to the media Guy could be in serious trouble. Before anyone knows of any possible treaty, they want the deal to be signed and sealed, with a peace-keeping force already on the island.'

Dion frowned. 'Why?'

'Because,' Luka said evenly, 'the neighbouring state is poised to march across the border and take over. They'll stay on the sidelines as long as they think the two sides are bleeding to death, but any hint of peace will see them invade. Guy is being kept three miles from the border on the main route to the capital city.'

Dion swore this time.

'Exactly,' his Prince said harshly. 'He's safe as long as no one knows anything about the possibility of a treaty between the Sant'Rosa rebels and the government.'

'So what do we do?' Dion asked, crisp and professional.

Luka said deliberately, 'From what I heard last night, the rebels won't be too hard to persuade—especially if they're promised a place in the new order of things. The government has guaranteed this. I've put out feelers amongst the local refugees from Sant'Rosa—apparently there are several with direct links to the rebels.' He looked at Dion, recognising the other man's frustration and need for action. 'Make sure the jet's ready to fly— we may need to airlift them into Auckland and take them up to the beach house. Apart from that, you'll do nothing—yet.' He smiled ironically. 'And before I start work on a peace plan that will satisfy both sides, I plan to swim.'

Dion said, 'Guy is tough, Luka. He'll probably get himself out of there.'

Luka gave a crooked smile. 'I know.' He paused and said abruptly, 'There is something else you can do. Make sure Alexa Mytton is not permitted into the hotel until after the conference is over.'

Although he turned up the jets in the private pool to full power, swimming didn't clear his mind. Instead of working out a way to free his cousin, or bring both bitterly divided sides to a neutral meeting place, all he wanted was to feel Alexa's hair around him like some silken tent, each coiling tress caressing his skin into feverish ecstasy. He wanted her to look at him with her ice-clear dangerous eyes smouldering with desire, in the full knowledge of what she was doing. He wanted to feel that passionate mouth on his skin...

He hauled himself out of the pool and strode towards the shower, sweat gathering on his forehead as his body responded to the goad of his thoughts.

More than anything in the world he craved to take her, bury himself deeply in her strong slenderness, mark her by his possession so that any other man's touch on her would be unthinkable—an insult, an unbearable horror.

Because he was fastidious—and circumspect—there hadn't been many women in his bed, but without conceit he knew he was a good lover. Partly it was his true appreciation of women's needs, his pleasure in their softness and their curves, his understanding that making love was an infinitely greater risk for a woman than for a man. But it was the self-mastery taught to him by the courtesan his father had summoned as a sixteenth birthday present that brought his lovers to sobbing fulfilment before he yielded to his own climax.

And it was that control that enabled him to keep himself emotionally distant from each one. He'd been trained in a hard school to think of his country before anything else.

Yet now he'd been ambushed by a hunger that clamoured to take a woman hot-bloodedly and without finesse, loosen control and let mindless white-hot passion ride him to satiety.

A photographer, for God's sake! And sniffing around now, at the very worst of times. One hint of publicity and the desperate men he'd met last night would disappear out of New Zealand and back into their tropical jungle, and more people would die, more children would grow up uneducated, knowing only war and famine and disease.

And Guy, his younger cousin, could well lose his life.

With a quick, savage flick of his fingers he turned the shower onto full, and when that didn't tame his rampant body he punched the palm of one hand with a clenched fist and fought the dangerous frustration with hard common sense.

Where had he seen those astonishing eyes before, so pale they were almost transparent, their colour a violent contrast to her warm Mediterranean colouring of creamy skin and copper hair?

A knock on the door brought his head up. 'What is it?' he asked with harsh precision.

'A message, sir,' his private secretary said urgently. 'The one you've been waiting for.'

That night, as she cooked dinner and ate it without tasting a mouthful, Alexa replayed over and over again that scene with Prince Luka.

It didn't take a psychologist to explain the electricity that had scorched through her at his touch. She'd been caught off guard by potent physical attraction, the kind of sensual intuition that splintered the bars of caution and common sense to whisper alluringly of feverish, compelling sex, to counsel surrender to a passion she'd never expected to feel.

Basic, earthy, almost entirely amoral, it should repel her. Emotionally and intellectually it did.

Unfortunately some rash, previously unsuspected part of her found Prince Luka wildly exciting. He'd kissed her like a conqueror, and she'd let him—worse than that, she'd gloried in it, because she'd known she'd breached some barrier in him.

Even more intriguing was that hint of vulnerability, of hidden secrets. Perhaps she could do some research on him—

'No!' she said, outraged.

And she should stop beating herself up! It wasn't as though she was the first woman to have found him attractive. Every magazine and newspaper in the western world was a witness to the number of women who'd fallen for his particular brand of Mediterranean glamour. And as well as being dynamically sexy, he'd been surprisingly kind when she'd started falling to pieces.

The telephone rang. 'Alexa,' Carole said in a flat voice, 'something's happened that's rather—upsetting.'

CHAPTER THREE

'I'VE just been speaking to Mike, my boss,' Carole said, with no sign of her usual dramatic delivery. 'He's suggested that you be—that you're not...' She hesitated before continuing bluntly, 'Alexa, he doesn't want to see you in the hotel for the duration of the conference.'

Stunned, Alexa asked, 'What? Why? He can't do that!' But he would, she realised with a clutch of nausea, if someone with enough power asked him to.

'I'm afraid he can, and I'm also afraid I must ask you not to lose your temper and try to force your way in,' Carole said, dropping her tone by several notes.

'Of course I won't embarrass you like that.' Alexa steadied her words. 'I'm just—gobsmacked. Did your boss give you a reason?'

'He was told officially that you're a photographer,' Carole said, 'and at the moment photographers are very much *personae non gratae*. Of course I vouched for your integrity, and pointed out that you'd worked here before and that you had security clearance. Mike knows that, but he's in a cleft stick; he said it's temporary, and no reflection on you.'

Fighting a raw sense of betrayal, Alexa unclenched her jaw with difficulty and ignored the faint questioning note in the older woman's voice to say, 'Carole, it's all right. As it happens I've got a full programme for the next week, so I probably wouldn't have been able to do anything for you anyway.'

Carole sighed, a sure sign of her panache returning.

'Thanks for being so understanding. A model tried to sweet-talk her way into the Prince of Dacia's suite yesterday—and almost got there. Apparently she sold a story to an English paper. Management is stressing out collectively and individually over security, so when someone said you were a photographer it was the final straw.'

And Alexa knew who that had to be! The Prince of Dacia was no slouch when it came to quick, ruthless decisions. She said brightly, 'Don't worry, I'll keep well away from the hotel. Are there likely to be any repercussions for you?'

'Me? Oh, no. Alexa, Mike *knows* you're trustworthy,' Carole assured her earnestly. 'He's under pressure from someone, and you can't blame that someone. It's just a pity you're the one to suffer. I have to go, Alexa. Thanks.'

After carefully putting the telephone down, Alexa strode furiously across to her window and threw it open. Salty air from the harbour, almost overwhelmed by petrol fumes, floated in, bringing with it all the noises of the city.

Talk about brutal misuse of power! she thought vengefully. How she'd like to tell Prince Luka of Dacia what she thought of people who used their status to intimidate.

A glance at her watch revealed that she had half an hour to go the gym and work off both her temper and the stupid, baseless sense of bereavement that kept breaking through.

She was a modern woman and Luka Bagaton was fresh out of the Middle Ages—protective of the weak, impersonally kind, hard, ruthless and chauvinist to the core. They had nothing in common, so this unsuitable, reckless attraction would die as soon as it had sprung up.

A week later she folded the newspaper so she couldn't see the Prince, lethally aristocratic and authoritative amongst the other bankers in a final posed photograph on the museum steps. Buttering toast with a vicious sweep of the knife, she said to the empty kitchen, 'I wonder just how much being superbly photogenic has helped his career as a banker. Lots, I'll bet.'

A swift glance through the window revealed a mellow autumn day, perfect for travelling. She planned to touch up her tan for ten glorious days at the beach house owned by the parents of a schoolfriend on an island forty miles north of Auckland. She had it all organised: days of glorious solitude stalking the perfect shot that was going to win her a competition.

Still chewing toast and honey, she cast a cold glance at the newspaper. The morning after that icy interview with the Prince the gossip columnist had struck again wondering archly:

What is going on between gorgeous Prince Luka and the lovely photographer? The same little bird that saw them together on the first night of the conference noticed the photographer emerging from the Prince's private elevator with tumbled hair and distinctly bee-stung lips. Watch this space!

So by now he'd be convinced she was feeding the wretched woman information.

Not that Alexa cared. 'Not even the tiniest bit,' she said, smiling brilliantly—and lying.

The island, she decided three hours later, manoeuvring

her friends' elderly four-wheel drive vehicle over the
narrow winding track from Deep Harbour, was the ideal
place to blob out—and to chisel a dangerously magnetic
man out of her brain.

The Thorntons had sited their bach on the ocean side
of the island, more exposed to the waves and the winds
than the gentler leeward side. That fitted Alexa's mood
perfectly, as did the comfortable middle-aged house
crouched above a sweeping beach with sand the colour
of fine champagne.

And the forecasters were predicting that the weather
would stay in Indian summer mode until after she returned to Auckland.

Determined to enjoy herself, Alexa opened glass doors
to let in the air, turned on the power and the water, and
began to unload the vehicle. That done, she rang Sally
Thornton in Auckland to tell her she'd arrived safely.

Then she ran down the beach for a quick dip to wash
off the road grime. At last, clad in denim shorts and a
sleeveless blue-green T-shirt that gave some colour to
her eyes, she strolled out onto the deck and stared out
to sea.

'Not another house in sight,' she said with satisfaction. The ruinous farmhouse along the beach, crouched
defensively behind thick old trees, didn't count.

Smiling, she dragged a lounger out onto the deck and
squinted along the bay, mentally framing at least three
superb shots. Tomorrow she'd go out and see what else
she could find. She wanted to play with black and white
shots.

Out of nowhere sprang the image of Luka's face when
he'd accused her of leaking gossip to the press—a face
with the kind of hard, forceful bone structure that photographed magnificently.

'Oh, for heaven's sake,' she muttered in frustration.

Absurdly sensitive to beauty she might be, but it was ridiculous to obsess about a man she'd only seen three times. OK, so he kissed like a dark angel, but punishing kisses had gone out with her mother's generation. No, her grandmother's!

Alexa grinned suddenly, recalling her grandmother—bright, modern, and tough enough to be a solo parent when it would have been a lot easier to put her son up for adoption. Gran would have had no truck with punishing kisses either. Her smile faded swiftly as loneliness rolled over her in a dark tide.

Her happy, charmed life, so safe and secure, had come to a bitter end. Her mother had died after a long illness when Alexa was just fourteen; two days previously, on the way home from the hospital, Alexa had been the only survivor of a motorway accident that had killed her father and grandmother. Stunned with grief, and left without relatives, Alexa had spent the rest of her school years in a foster home.

Yet, unlike some of the others there, she'd had happy memories. Just what sort of memories haunted Luka of Dacia, who'd admitted to imbibing distrust with his mother's milk?

'Get out of my head!' Alexa commanded the man who'd had her dismissed like a dishonest servant.

Late that night, woken from a deep sleep by something she'd barely heard, she pulled on a woollen jersey against the chilly air and made her way out onto the deck. The timeless silhouette of the hills brooding against the night sky and the subtle obsidian sheen of the sea beneath the stars usually satisfied something deep in her soul, but not tonight. The warm glow from the small lamp in the sitting room beckoned much more strongly.

She'd swung around to go inside again when a point of light stopped her. Adrenalin powered up her pulse-rate by several beats a minute. No one had lived in the old house along the beach since the owner had been forced to spend his final years on the mainland.

'Well, someone's there now,' she said aloud, then froze as a noise from the sea boosted her heart into over-drive. With night-attuned eyes she made out the shape of a large launch in the bay; the sound she'd heard was the creak of oars as someone rowed ashore.

Nothing unusual in that, but she stayed motionless until the autumn chill drove her inside.

Unable to pin down the source of her uneasiness, she retired back to bed, this time locking the door onto the deck. Probably the neighbouring property had changed hands, but there was a possibility—so remote it was barely worth considering—that someone had broken into the house and was lying low.

The next morning the peacock waters of the bay spread out a gleaming, serene emptiness beneath the sun. Brows knitting, Alexa rang Sally in Auckland.

'Oh, I forgot to tell you!' her friend said cheerfully. 'After Mr Patrick died it was sold to some millionaire who demolished the old house and built a very upmarket bach there. Well, not a bach—more a mansion! He's got riparian rights to half the cove, but I don't think he's ever stayed there. I suppose he bought it as an invest-ment.'

Amused at the mindset of anyone buying land in such a glorious place for that prosaic reason, Alexa said cheerfully, 'He seems to be in residence at the moment because I saw a light there last night.'

'That'll be from the caretaker's house a bit further along. A nice middle-aged couple—you'll like them if you meet them.'

So much for night-time uneasiness—the launch in the bay the previous night had probably ferried the caretaker back from a fishing trip! Five minutes later, a small pack over her shoulders, Alexa pushed a hat onto her head, donned her sunglasses and picked up her father's old camera. Time to go exploring.

Halfway along the pale curve of the beach a soft scrabble in the scrub froze her into stillness. Wallabies, brought across the Tasman Sea more than a century ago by one of the original settlers, could sometimes be seen hopping along the sand, lending the beach a bizarre Australian air. A gap in the teatree scrub might indicate a track.

Narrowing her eyes, she checked the light. Perfect, and with the splendid iconic pohutukawa tree in the background it would make a surreal image.

Slowly and silently she eased herself behind a large wave-smoothed rock and readied the camera.

After ten minutes of motionless waiting with the sun radiating off the rock, Alexa itched in several places and longed for a drink. Experience warned her that any hiding wallaby would decide to hop down onto the beach at the exact moment she reached for her water, only to be spooked into cover by her movement.

The back of her neck prickled. Concentrating ferociously, she stopped herself from glancing behind.

No small grey animal emerged onto the beach. Sunlight sizzled across sand tinted pinky-gold by the fragments of millions of shells, and shimmered in fascinating patterns over lazy, glassy waves. A gull shrieked from behind her—probably defending some choice titbit. Camera at the ready, Alexa fought an eerie feeling of being watched.

Finally she could stand it no longer. Patiently, carefully, she turned her head.

And looked straight up into eyes of frozen fire—contemptuous eyes in a handsome, autocratic face. Her heart crashed against her breastbone; instinctively she jumped sideways, and the camera dropped from her numb fingers onto the rock as she fought to keep her balance.

An iron grip stopped her from falling ignominiously onto her face and set her on her feet in the yielding sand. 'Are you hurt?' Prince Luka of Dacia demanded.

'I'm all right.' Fighting for control, she twisted away from hands that opened instantly and let her go. She dropped to one knee to pick up the camera case, catching back a small cry of dismay as it flexed ominously.

'What the hell are you doing?' Luka asked with harsh distinctness. 'This is private property.'

'But not *your* private property. I have every right to be here.' Astonished by the flood of sheer physical excitement that threatened to overwhelm her, Alexa stood up, clutching the shattered camera and lifting her head to stare aggressively at his wide, straight, alarmingly sensual mouth. 'You're the trespasser, not me.'

His hard handsome face froze.

Recklessly Alexa pushed her luck. 'So, what are *you* doing here?'

For a second he looked dangerously close to losing his cool. Perversely, Alexa hoped he would. It seemed only fair. He'd scared the life out of her, startled her into smashing her father's camera—one of the few mementoes she had of him—then had the nerve to look at her as though she were a slug in his lettuce.

'I am on holiday,' he said in a tone that could have sliced granite.

Alexa struggled with the impulse to tell him to go to hell. 'So am I,' she stated, her hand clenching over the camera case. When something jabbed her finger she fought back sudden bleak tears as she jerked it away.

'What's the matter?'

'Nothing,' she snapped.

But he'd seen the blood. Saying something short and untranslatable in the musical language that was presumably Dacian, he stooped and caught her hand, lifting it to examine the cut. 'Is the glass still in there?'

'The lens isn't broken,' she muttered, the small pain vanquished by the sudden uproar of her senses. How could one man's touch cause such mayhem? 'It's just a cut from the shards of the case.'

Luka hauled a handkerchief from his pocket and mopped the bead of blood away. Black brows drawn together in a formidable frown, he checked the cut carefully before wrapping the cloth around her finger. Then he looked up.

And caught her watching him.

He returned her gaze with flinty eyes reflecting the shimmer of the sun on the sea. 'Where is your boat?'

'Boat?' Bemused by the jumble of sensations rioting through her, Alexa said, 'What boat?'

Although his fingers didn't tighten around her wrist, she knew she didn't have a chance of pulling free.

Ice-cold, he said, 'The one you arrived on.'

'The only boat around here is the one that came into the bay last night—the big launch I presume you arrived on. I came by car—a four-wheel drive, actually.'

Silence—taut, stark and thrumming with unspoken words—stretched between them. The sun swathed gold over his skin, highlighting stark cheekbones and gleaming golden eyes half hidden by heavy lids and long lashes. He appeared to be thinking hard and fast. With silky indolence he pointed out, 'This is an island, Alexa.'

'I know it's an island.'

Insultingly, relentlessly polite, he asked, 'So how did you manage to reach this beach by car?'

She retorted with frosty hauteur, 'You have no right to cross-question me.'

'Answer me.' *Or we'll stay here all day.* His tone and the implacable cast of his features said the words for him.

Chills skimmed the length of her spine. For the first time Alexa realised how vulnerable she was, alone on a lonely beach with a man who paid the salaries of the nearest people. Not far beneath Luka's sophisticated surface lurked a warrior, with a warrior's outlook, formidable and ruthlessly practical.

But this was New Zealand! He was the interloper here, not her.

She said crisply, 'I drove to the Spit, left my car in the car park, caught the ferry to Deep Harbour and picked up the four-wheel drive my friends keep garaged there. Then I drove over the island to my friends' bach.' She jerked her head backwards. 'Along the beach. And you, I conclude, are the millionaire next door?'

Hooded eyes narrowed further into smouldering chips. 'I'm certainly next door.'

With Sandra Beauchamp?

Angry with him for interrogating her—but furious at the incandescent, unwilling response of her body to his touch—Alexa twisted her wrist away.

Luka's fingers relaxed instantly, although he didn't

step back. Instead he watched with narrowed eyes as she unwound his handkerchief and examined her finger.

'It's stopped bleeding,' she said practically. Her voice sounded as prosaic as the words, which was a relief, because her tense body was humming with adrenalin, ready to run. Or surrender…

Ignoring that degrading thought, Alexa stooped to pick up the other small shards of plastic from the destroyed camera case. When she'd recovered every one she could see, she dropped them into his immaculate handkerchief. Well, immaculate except for the scarlet stain of her blood. Carefully she flicked the last dark splinter into the white linen and tied the handkerchief into a loose knot.

Luka said conversationally, 'I'm surprised you use such an old camera.' His voice altered. 'What have I said?'

With an inelegant sniff that didn't hide the dampness in her eyes, Alexa said truculently, 'It was my father's. He—he was interested in photography—he bought me my first camera and when he died I—I managed to salvage this one.' She bit her lip to stem any further confidences.

'Salvage it from what?' Luka asked in a deeper, gentler voice.

Unwillingly she told him, 'When my parents died I was sent to a foster home. The government organisation that cared for me sold everything we owned except for my things and a couple of mementoes.'

'How old were you?' he asked.

'Fourteen.' She looked down at the little parcel of plastic.

He said quietly, 'I was fourteen when my mother died.'

Alexa looked up sharply and surprised a fleeting expression on his handsome face that twisted her heart. 'Not a good year for losing parents,' she said wryly, adding, 'At least you had your father.'

'I don't suppose any year is a good year to lose a parent.' Luka looked past her to the Thorntons' bach. 'How long are you staying?'

His patent eagerness to get rid of her was like a slap in the face. For a moment there she'd thought they'd achieved a tenuous understanding. Shrugging, she said, 'Ten days. It doesn't matter, you know—I'll stay out of your way. You can always avoid me by swimming in the pool up at the house instead of off the beach—the rip can be dangerous.'

'Been snooping, Alexa?' he asked silkily, heavy lashes hooding his eyes.

'No need to,' she returned, chilled yet defiant. 'Millionaires always have pools. It's part of the mindset— like paranoia.' And arrogance.

Schooling her face into an expression of calm dismissal, she held out the handkerchief with its bloodstain and its little cargo of plastic.

Angular features tough and forbidding, he stood motionless. Sharp fierce tension throbbed between them while the waves crisped against the sand and the sun beat down, hot and heavy as summer, summoning blue from the black depths of Luka's hair and lovingly outlining the compelling angles and planes of his face. Alexa fought an impulse to run.

Even when at last he took the handkerchief from her she couldn't relax.

He said levelly, 'I want privacy, Alexa. I'd be happy to organise a holiday for you somewhere else—Hawaii, northern Australia, the Islands. England in the spring is very beautiful.'

Good resolutions forgotten, she returned with a steely fury she'd later think ridiculous, 'I don't want to go anywhere else. I'm perfectly happy here.' Flicking her hair back from her suddenly hot face, she said with a taunting smile, 'Perhaps you could get a stick and draw a line down the beach on the boundary. I promise I won't cross it.'

The silence that followed those unwise words was as brittle as the case of her father's camera, until Luka said, 'But how much can I trust your promise?'

Alexa knew she'd regret letting her normally even temper get the better of her, but at this moment it exhilarated her. Coolly defiant, she said, 'Enjoy the rest of your stay in New Zealand.' With a brisk little air she held out her hand.

After a moment Luka's long fingers closed around hers, lifting them so that he could kiss the little cut. Thick black lashes half hid his metallic eyes, and as his mouth branded her skin Alexa crossed a hidden boundary into wild, unknown territory.

But it wasn't until he turned her hand over and bit it delicately on the fleshy mound beneath her thumb that her body went crazy.

She yanked her hand back and stared at him. White-faced, grabbing for composure, she said shakily, 'Is that how you say goodbye in Dacia?'

'That's how we say *I want you very much* in Dacia,' he drawled. 'Why look so shocked? You already knew that.' Unforgivably he finished, 'And you want me too. I hope you find it as irritating as I do.'

Alexa could have kicked herself for giving him such an opening. She swallowed. 'I'm going. Goodbye.'

His laugh was low and unamused, totally cynical. 'I think we'll see each other again.'

'Not if I see you first,' she shot back, and set off for the bach.

Marching steadily along the beach, she could feel his gaze bore into her shoulders. What had been an enjoyable five-minute walk half an hour ago now seemed to take hours, and by the time she reached the house she was parched and slightly dizzy.

'So drink your water next time,' she said staunchly, shrugging out of her pack and opening the bottle in it. She drained the slightly warm liquid and set the bottle down with a small defiant crash.

Luka of Dacia might want her but he certainly didn't like her. Well, that was entirely mutual.

Of all the wretched coincidences! And why hadn't she been able to keep a guard on her tongue?

Every time she saw him the devastating impact of his sexuality burned away her confidence. Like some dark enchanter he paralysed her common sense and her will-power and sent her hormones crazy.

'It's quite simple. You're a strongly visual person,' she rationalised, 'and heaven knows he's got enough good looks to stock a model agency. Of course he affects you—you'd be a lousy photographer if he didn't.'

So why not leave the island?

Because that would be ceding some sort of victory to him in this intense, irrational war they were fighting. If she tamely gave up and ran away she'd be surrendering.

Dion watched his Prince stride across the room and come to a halt in the window. 'So what do you plan to do?' he asked in a neutral voice.

'I have no choice,' Luka said harshly. 'Alexa Mytton

will want to keep our whereabouts as quiet as she can so that she can earn the utmost from her photographs and copy, but if she does let slip that we're here the bay will be crawling with paparazzi within hours. Last night the Sant'Rosans revealed that they've been having discussions with the New Zealand government, who are prepared to send a peace-keeping force as soon as an accord is signed, but until then they want secrecy. Guy will be in real danger if news of those meetings gets out.'

'Only if we don't get to him first,' Dion said urgently.

'If we make an attempt to rescue him we can give up any chance of peace there,' Luka said, an austere note hardening his voice into grimness. 'I understand what it is not to trust anyone.'

Which was why he couldn't let this ridiculous hunger for a flame-haired beauty stand in his way.

Forcing himself to ignore the persistent clamour of his senses, he went on, 'If Alexa Mytton is not paparazzi she has links with them, and I won't risk my cousin's life for a pair of brilliant eyes.' And a body that still tormented his dreams. He gave a hard, unamused smile. 'As my father used to say, "Never trust anyone. And especially never trust a woman."'

'It's a cynical creed to live by,' Dion observed, watching him closely.

'One that works.' To save his island realm from invasion his father had married the only child of the dictator poised to crush Dacian freedom. He'd sired her child, and in the fifteen years of their marriage he'd never trusted her.

Repressing memories of the quiet, weary woman who had loved him, Luka said, 'I might give Ms Mytton the benefit of the doubt if it weren't for the other items of gossip in that damned column. As it is, I dare not. I can't permit her to tell anyone I am here.'

'I agree,' Dion said, nodding. 'So, to get back to the point, what are you going to do?'

Luka shrugged. 'Whatever I have to,' he said in a flat, lethal voice.

'Trust the Sant'Rosans?'

'Oh, no,' Luka said coolly. 'You will organise a group to snatch Guy; get them as close to Sant'Rosa as you can, without alerting the islanders, and tell them to wait until you contact them before doing anything.'

Dion nodded. 'And what about Ms Mytton?'

'Run another, more complete check on her. I want to know everything—friends, family, professional standing, lovers. Bank account.'

A knock at the door turned both men's heads. 'Come in,' Luka said.

A stolid, middle-aged man entered and bowed. 'Your Highness,' he said after Luka had greeted him. 'The woman is taking pictures.'

Luka's stomach contracted, as though warding off a blow. Angry at this sign of weakness, he asked, 'Of what?' surprised that his voice stayed so level.

'Of the sand, and some birds, but mostly along the beach.'

Luka exchanged glances with his head of security before saying, 'Thank you. Go back and continue watching.'

The man hesitated and Dion asked, 'What is it?'

'I think perhaps I was careless and let the sun catch the lens of my binoculars,' he said apologetically.

Dion said sternly, 'Make sure it doesn't happen again.'

The man saluted and sketched another bow before disappearing.

'I'll pay another visit to Ms Mytton,' Luka said with a flat, deadly intensity. He sensed he'd startled the other man, but he was gripped by a disappointment that consumed him until he could barely breathe. Somehow the spirited, fiery Alexa Mytton had got to him so hard he couldn't think clearly for wanting her.

Never, since that first treacherous affair, had he wanted to trust a woman so much. Well, that was a lesson he'd learned very well.

CHAPTER FOUR

ALEXA removed the film from the camera, telling herself sternly that by obsessing about the man she was giving him power over her.

She didn't care about Prince Luka. 'Not at all,' she said aloud. He was someone from another world, a glamorous, exotic world where duty meant everything and love nothing. She knew exactly what she wanted in life—a satisfying career, a man she could love, and children. A family to replace the one torn so brutally from her, and an ordinary life with all the ordinary pleasures and some, certainly, of the ordinary pain.

Luka was far from ordinary.

But when a thickening of the atmosphere pulled her head around and she saw his big, lean body silhouetted in the door a shameful flare of anticipation shortened her breath and pulled every tiny hair on her skin upright. She'd rather cross swords with this man than kiss another.

Clutching the container of film, she said bluntly, 'I didn't hear you knock.'

'I didn't, and I'm not waiting for an invitation to come inside either.' He walked in and glanced around with the searching concentration she'd seen on the news from those anonymous men whose job it was to take bullets for their masters. As well as the room, that hard, swift survey took in her camera on the table, the film in her hand, and the special bag she kept her other films in.

'You're quite safe,' she said evenly, suppressing a

59

shaft of sympathy. No one should have to live like that, wondering who was aiming what at them. 'No hidden photographers waiting to pounce.'

'How about hidden cameras?'

'No,' she said shortly. 'Why should there be? To what do I owe the pleasure...' her voice lingered with delicate scorn on the word '...of this visit?'

His eyes narrowed. 'I came to this island for a private holiday. I know that you have links to whoever writes that gossip column, and are a friend of the hotel events manager. Naturally I find your presence here suspicious.'

Did he suspect Carole? Chin jutting, Alexa said, 'Besides being excellent at her job, Carole Molloy is a consummate professional—she wouldn't tip off a gossip columnist.'

'I didn't say she had.'

'You insinuated it! Carole doesn't deserve to be blamed for—'

He interrupted her with a hint of cynicism. 'You're very loyal.'

'She was good to me when I needed help,' Alexa said fiercely, 'and she has nothing to do with any of this.'

'That doesn't matter now,' he said, dismissing Carole with a careless arrogance that set Alexa's teeth on edge. 'She is no longer a player. You, however, are.'

'All I want is to spend a peaceful holiday taking photographs for a competition!' Alexa told him stonily. 'I am not—repeat not, not, *not*—interested in you or whoever you have visiting you!'

Again that dangerous hooded glance, keen and lethal as the blade of a golden dagger, contrasting with the calm pleasantness of his tone when he said, 'I don't trust you, Alexa Mytton. I don't believe in coincidences, especially when they concern journalists. One item in a gossip column could be bad luck. Two are extremely suspicious, and three—'

'Three?' Alexa echoed, startled.

'Three times. Yesterday she mentioned that you and I were spending time together on a romantic island tryst.'

Alexa's mouth fell open. 'I don't believe it.' Her mind raced over people who might possibly have known where she was going—only her friends, and they certainly wouldn't be talking to any gossip columnist.

'I can show you the newspaper if you want to check it,' he said with exquisite contemptuous politeness.

Biting her lip, Alexa said, 'No, if you say it's there, I believe you. But that lets Carole off the hook. She didn't know I was coming here.'

'I've already told you I am no longer interested in Carole Molloy.' He waited, but when Alexa remained silent, he went on, 'I want any films you've exposed. And I won't pay you for them. I despise blackmailers.'

'And I despise bullies. I don't know how on earth that wretched columnist knows where I am,' Alexa sputtered, still stunned, 'but I am not in the business of selling spy shots—not even of you, not even if you stripped naked in front of me!'

His eyes gleamed. 'No matter how much you were offered for it?'

'No,' she retorted.

'Do professional photographers habitually try to kiss their way out of trouble?' he asked, watching her with an intent, unsettling gaze.

The blatant unfairness of this set fire to her temper. '*You* kissed *me*.'

'It was an experiment. You had only to resist and I'd have let you go. You didn't resist,' he said coolly, watching her with hard, analytical eyes. 'Why?'

An *experiment*! The colour faded from Alexa's face, leaving her clammy and furious. He was right, damn him. She was the one who'd lost it, totally and embarrassingly, responding to him with all the fervour of a schoolgirl kissed by her first love.

Thanks to a temper she hadn't known she possessed until she met this dictatorial man, things were way out of control. Time to try calm reason. Summoning a cool smile, she said, 'Whatever, that's got nothing to do with photography, which is my job and my passion.'

'What were you doing down on the beach?'

'Trying to catch the difference between summer and autumn.' His raised brows persuaded her to continue, 'I'm intrigued by the subtle variations in seasons. An autumn day can be almost as hot as a summer's one, but there is a difference in—in texture, and one of these days I'll catch that difference on film.'

A mocking lift of his brows revealed that he didn't believe a word. 'We can do this easily or with difficulty.'

She stared mutinously at him. 'Easily for whom?' she demanded crisply.

His smile was worldly and ironic. 'Give me any cameras you have, plus films, with a promise not to take any more. They'll be returned to you when you leave.'

'And the easy way?' she asked, winged black brows shooting up above pale, seething eyes.

He laughed abruptly. 'That *is* the easy way. If you refuse I'll have you kept under guard.'

Furiously, she scanned the speculative amusement in Luka's face as he watched her search for words.

When she'd recovered enough to speak, she said calmly and coldly, 'This is New Zealand, not your own private fiefdom. If you so much as lay a finger on me I'll see you in court on a charge of assault, and not even being a prince will be enough to save you from that here. New Zealand is a democracy.'

'So is Dacia,' he said, bored. 'As for touching you...' His gaze swept her mouth.

Heat fountained through her, fire to match his smouldering gaze. Her breasts tightened and became heavy, the nipples thrusting urgently at the thin cotton over them.

'Who would believe you?' he asked softly, surveying her with a flick of contempt. 'You respond so vividly to me that I'd have no problem convincing any enquirers that you came away with me and then tried to blackmail me into paying you off. You'd get your day of notoriety—possibly even some money from the gutter press— but if you *are* a serious photographer you'd lose all credibility.'

Alexa made a small panicky movement, then lifted her head proudly. 'You wouldn't dare.'

He shrugged. 'I would,' he said softly, and she believed him. His voice changed, deepened, and his smile, free of anything but warm, ironic humour, hit her like a blow to her heart.

'Alexa, privacy is important to me. Can you not simply enjoy your time here without taking photographs?'

She recognised calculated charm when she saw it, but even then it washed over her like a sensual tide and she wanted to surrender, give him what he wanted. Contracting every muscle in her body, she said, 'I do understand—I think—how angry and frustrated media attention must make you, and I can see why you're suspicious—'

'So you do accept that I have reason to be?'

Where had that wretched columnist got her information from? 'I've just said I do. But I have as much right to be here as you. You have my word that I won't take any photographs of you.' Drawing a long bow, she added grandly, 'Or your guests. Please go now.' She turned away.

He reached her in two strides, stopping her with a firm grip around her upper arm. Before she could react, he seized the hand clutching the canister and forced her fingers apart. The little container toppled, was caught with another of those swift movements, and she was free. Outraged, Alexa launched herself at him, only to be held away with one strong, merciless hand.

'You are an intransigent woman,' he said harshly as he flicked off the top and shook out the reel.

'No,' Alexa cried, abandoning her retaliation when she realised that he intended to expose it to the light.

Grim-faced, he paused. 'Creative anguish?' he drawled, eyes as cold and hard as crystals, searching her horrified face. 'Or the prospect of losing a lot of money?'

Alexa opened her mouth, but before she could speak he went on with brusque irritation, 'All right, I'll get them developed first.'

'You are so kind,' Alexa raged, knowing it was futile, knowing she didn't have a hope of getting her film back. How she wished she'd taken self-defence lessons! Nothing would give her greater pleasure than to severely hurt him.

Cold logic told her that, attack training or not, she wouldn't have had a hope. Luka had moved with the lethal speed and skill of a professional warrior, using just enough strength to keep her away from the film, and even now he was watching her, ready to counter any attempt on her part to get it back.

Alexa knew when she was beaten. In a low, tense

voice she said, 'One day you're going to pay for that, I promise you. Now you've got what you came for, get out.'

'Not before I collect any other cameras,' he said.

'By the time I've finished with you, you'll be in prison for years!'

'I doubt it,' he said tersely. 'But unless you let me take your photographic equipment I'll send one of those minions you're so scathing about down to search the house.'

'I'd prefer that,' she retorted. 'At least he'd be just doing his job.'

'Is that what you want?'

She hesitated, then said reluctantly, 'No.'

'So show me your cameras.'

Furiously she said, 'This is the only other one I have here, and if you break it too I'll—'

He said forcibly, 'I won't break it. And I want any unexposed films you might have.'

Alexa bared her teeth. 'Get them yourself.'

Lips clamped together, she watched him pick up the bag and glance into it.

'I will of course return them,' he said courteously. 'And now I need your mobile telephone.'

Of course. If she had been a journalist, the mobile phone would be a logical way of dictating copy or sending text messages. It was sitting in full view on the bookcase, but she was damned if she was going to meekly hand it to him.

'Get it yourself.' Recklessly Alexa pushed her luck. 'I'm not your servant, so don't expect me to curtsy and run around after you.'

'You're not my subject,' he said, in a tone that could

have sliced granite, 'so nothing more formal than a handshake is expected.'

She waited until he'd slid the phone into the breast pocket of his well-cut shirt before saying with brittle precision, 'I ring my friend every morning.'

'Then every morning I will come down with the telephone so that you can speak to her,' he said courteously. 'Unfortunately I will need to listen in to the conversation.'

Alexa sent him a glittering glance. 'It will be a pleasant constitutional for you.'

He smiled, but went on, 'Do you have a computer?'

'Yes.' He paused, and she said truculently, 'There are no telephone lines into the bach, so I can't send anything out.'

'Why did you bring it?'

She flushed. 'It's none of your business.'

'But you will tell me just the same,' he said with silky menace.'

Alexa shrugged. 'All right, I'm using software I've just bought to fill in details of my family tree.'

His frown dissipating, he said, 'That's an unusual hobby for one so young.'

Bestowing a smile edged with mockery on him, she said sweetly, 'For those whose family history is well-documented, perhaps it is, but mine is not. And because I'm the only one left on my particular branch of the family tree, I'm very interested in finding out if there are any others.'

'You are completely alone in the world?'

She lifted her chin. 'I've got friends.' *Which,* she allowed her tone to imply, *is more than you have.*

His brows drew together. 'You're bleeding!'

As she followed his gaze to her hand he dumped her

gear onto the table and strode across the room to where she stood. Their tussle for the film had opened the small cut in her finger, releasing a thin line of blood.

Colour heated Luka's arrogantly defined cheekbones. 'I'm sorry,' he said in a rough voice, 'I didn't mean to hurt you.' And as though compelled he lifted her hand to his mouth and sucked the tiny bead.

Alexa gave a choked gasp, her entire world narrowing to the intense pleasure his mouth called into life inside her.

Returning to sanity, she jerked her hand free, but it was too late; he caught her close and looked into her eyes with a fierce stare that claimed something from her.

Rash excitement burned away the last fragment of common sense in Alexa. The word he crushed against her lips was his name, and she melted into him, adrift and lost in uncharted seas.

If the first kisses had been dynamite, this one was a volcano, she thought dizzily. But she'd think about that later...

When he lifted his head she was so far gone that her mouth unconsciously followed his, seeking a return of the heady magic.

He laughed softly and his arms tightened about her, bringing her even closer to his tense, fully roused body.

'What is it you want?' he asked, heavy-lidded eyes promising unimaginable sensual pleasure, while the lazy note in his voice told her that he knew exactly what she wanted—and what she was inviting if she didn't stop this right now.

Alexa brought all her will-power to bear, ruthlessly quashing the images her treacherous brain supplied only too eagerly. He had a nerve.

'I am not a toy to amuse you,' she snarled, twisting away from him.

He proved just how little the kiss meant to him by releasing her instantly.

Her body throbbing, she threw at him, 'If you think you can come in here, steal my belongings, threaten me and then kiss me into stupidity, think again. I'm not an idiot.'

Stiff with hauteur, he said, 'I do not force women. You wanted that kiss as much as I did.'

It wasn't *fair*! Alexa wanted to yell her fury at whatever malevolent fate had brought Prince Luka of Dacia into her peaceful life. Her hair felt as though she'd been caught in a lightning chamber, and every muscle ached with the tension of frustrated lust and a terrifying loss of control. She wanted to stamp and pound and break things, because in spite of everything her body still ached for him.

Instead she said in a tight, strained voice, 'You've got what you came to get. Now get out of here before I start throwing things.'

'I can't leave you like this.' His voice was deliberate, steady.

'I'm all *right*.'

He pushed up her chin and scanned her face with hard, unsparing eyes. Ignoring her protests, and the closed fist she punched into his solar plexus, he picked her up and put her into a chair, his big frame taut and determined.

'It serves you right,' he said savagely as she cradled her painful knuckles. It had been like attacking a rock. 'Of course I tightened the muscles there. Do you have bandages for that finger—some cream?'

Alexa unclenched her teeth enough to spit, 'No.'

'Then I'll bring some down.'

'No! I don't need anything from you.' She closed her fingers into another fist. 'It's just a cut—it'll heal.'

Another swathe of swarthy colour licked along his magnificent cheekbones. 'I'm sorry,' he said, as though she'd wrung the words from him. 'I don't normally behave like a clumsy savage.' He swung on his heel and strode into the kitchen.

Alexa watched his black head above the bar that cut off the kitchen from the living room, and realised that he was pouring her a glass of water. He was, she thought dazedly as she began to come down from the adrenalin high, a complex mixture—both protective and antagonistic. She watched him warily as he came across the room.

Half-closed eyes, grimly gold, surveyed her through a thick layer of black lashes. 'Here,' he said, handing over the glass. 'Drink it all down.'

The water slid cold and refreshing down her throat, easing it enough so that she could say, 'Thank you,' politely and hold out the glass.

He gave her another of those searching glances before, apparently satisfied, taking it back into the kitchen.

Alexa got to her feet and wooed calmness. Memories forced their way into her brain—the unconstrained strength of the arms that had held her, the heavy, driving beat of Luka's heart, and that tantalising, elusive scent. And his warmth, the feeling she'd had of being protected as well as bewitched.

From behind, Luka said, 'You look better—do you feel it?'

'Certainly,' she said with composure, turning to face him. 'You overreacted to my natural irritation with myself for consorting with the enemy.'

His laughter startled her. 'One thing I'll say for you,'

he said, collecting the camera and the bag of films with
an easy movement, 'you're not dull.'

Alexa gave him another fulminating look, refusing to
back down. 'Don't patronise me. Unfortunately,' she
said between her teeth, 'you are entirely predictable.'

'Enjoy your holiday,' he baited her with a sarcastic
courtesy that set her teeth even further on edge.

Childishly—a state he seemed able to inflict on her at
will, she decided savagely—she cleaned her teeth, scrub-
bing the taste of him out of her mouth. As she stripped
off her clothes to shower she thought he should find a
way to bottle his natural scent and sell it as a stimulant.

It was humiliating to be so helpless against his sexual
power; whenever he came into the room her will-power
fell to pieces as messily and comprehensively as a pav-
lova tossed onto the floor. Attacking her treacherous
body vigorously with soap, she wondered why she
hadn't bitten him when he'd kissed her. Her hands
slowed.

'Because it never occurred to you,' she said irritably.
'You went under without a murmur.' But she'd like to
bite that olive skin—and then lick the small mark—

'Oh, stop it,' she wailed, horrified. 'What am I going
to do about this man?'

Perhaps running back to Auckland would be sensible.
Her mouth compressed. No, that would be surrender. It
was time Luka of Dacia realised that the world hadn't
been constructed to suit him alone.

'So I'll stay here, but keep well away from him,' she
answered grimly, and got out her computer and the
sheets of information she wanted to transfer onto it.

Halfway through an afternoon of sheer stubbornness
and many mistakes, she realised that Luka had accepted
her word that she had no other cameras.

CHAPTER FIVE

ALEXA woke with panic kicking her in the stomach and the sound of a dull roar echoing through her mind. Wind howled around the eaves, and the first onset of a squall exploded like small bullets on the roof. She relaxed and snuggled under the duvet, drifting off to sleep again to the drama of the storm blowing in from the sea.

The following morning, however, after waking to a still, placid day gilded by sunshine and perfumed with freshly wet grass, she discovered that the bach had no electricity. Which meant no shower, no toast, no coffee...

Fortunately there was the sea, and the barbecue. Half an hour later, after a brisk dip, she ate a piece of bread and honey while watching a battered pan steam gently over the gas jets. She'd have to call the power board, and to do that she needed her telephone, but the first priority was caffeine.

She cast a glance over her shoulder, almost dropping the bread when she saw Luka, the dark prince himself, striding along the beach. In spite of her sternest commands, her heart began to race as he approached, formidably tall and dominating.

His brows rose when he took in the sight of the barbecue and the pan and her salty, slightly sticky wet hair. 'Breakfast al fresco?' he asked coolly.

'No power,' she told him, cloaked in the tatters of her composure.

His brows drew together. 'What happened?'

'I don't know.' She shrugged against the hard topaz gaze. 'I assume the wind last night brought the line down.'

He flicked out her mobile phone—*her* phone!—and punched a number into it. After speaking briefly and incomprehensibly in Dacian, he frowned at the answer, then turned it off and said levelly, 'Someone's going to check the line. In the meantime, you'd better come back with me.'

That macho protectiveness thing again! 'I'm fine,' she said immediately. She gestured at the simmering saucepan. 'I have all I need—coffee and bread and honey.'

'Very rustic.' He surveyed her with a glimmer of amusement that brought her chin up.

Their eyes clashed, hot fire versus pale ice, until the sound of gas hissing and spitting made her jump. Sure enough, the water in the saucepan had begun to boil over the sides and hiss onto the gas.

When Alexa had switched off the gas and poured the water onto the coffee grounds in another saucepan, she looked up to see Luka scanning the barely visible tops of two huge water tanks buried in the bank behind the bach. Of course he noted the piece of rope she'd used in a futile attempt to haul off the hatch.

Frowning, he said, 'I assume you've no water?'

'Not now I've used up what was in the electric jug, but I'll dip it out once I get the hatch off.'

'Leave it—it's far too heavy,' he said.

She kept her eyes firmly averted from his broad shoulders and tightly muscled arms. 'Perhaps you could haul it off.'

'I could,' he drawled, 'but why bother when I can offer you a hot shower and coffee made properly? Come over and have breakfast at my house.'

She gave him an insouciant smile. 'That's very kind of you, but, as you can see, I'm fine,' she said sweetly. 'And barbecue coffee has a taste all on its own.'

Luka lifted his brows, meeting her smile with one of his own—deadly in impact. 'In that case, why don't you offer me some while we find out what's caused the power cut?'

'I'd better ring my friend in Auckland first,' she said, not giving an inch. 'It's her bach—well, her parents'— so they'll need to be told what's happened.'

'It would be better to wait until we know what's happened to your power supply,' he said calmly. 'I still have electricity, so it must be something between here and the junction.'

Irritated by the good sense in this suggestion, Alexa nodded and turned away, giving the coffee grounds in the pot an unnecessary stir.

'Did you get your data transferred to the genealogy software?' he asked idly.

She gave an ironic smile. 'After I'd worked out how to do it, yes.'

'How did you end up being so singularly bereft of family?'

She hesitated before saying defensively, 'My mother was an orphan, and on my father's side my grandfather died young and my grandmother never remarried.' She was not going to tell him that her grandparents on her father's side had never married, her young Italian grandfather dying before he knew his lover was having his child. 'And my mother was ill for a couple of years. Dad took Gran and me to see her in hospital, and on the way back we got hit in a tanker pile-up on the motorway. They were killed instantly. It was just bad luck.'

'It sounds more like tragedy,' he said, his voice very deep.

Because she didn't want to like him at all, she said pertly, 'I suppose you come from a very large family.' And then, pink with embarrassment, recalled that although he was related to most of the royal houses of Europe he was as bereft of immediate family as her.

He shrugged. 'Several hundred distant cousins of varying degrees, but close to me only two.'

His voice had—not hardened, exactly, but become remote, a vocal *No Trespassing* sign. Rebuffed, Alexa turned away.

'What was life like in that foster home?' Luka probed.

Alexa stirred the coffee grounds again. 'The first one was not good, but—'

He said something under his breath, then asked quietly, 'How bad?'

Stupid tears stung her eyes as she shook her head. 'I just didn't get on with their kids. I fitted much better into the second one. They were kind, and most of the other kids were all right. They kept coming and going, but I—well, I was lucky. I knew my mother and father had loved me. It gave me something to cling to when things were bad. Most of the other kids didn't have that.'

'Yes,' he said simply. In a tone she didn't recognise he said, 'It's very important, that knowledge.'

Had his mother loved him? Or his wily, hard father?

He added, 'Your parents must have been delighted that they had a child as sunny and vital as you.'

Startled, she looked up. He was watching her with a hooded glance, not sombre or calculating or grim, but as though she was something new and unusual. Well, ordinary people probably *were* an unknown quantity to him!

Carefully keeping the grounds in the bottom of the saucepan, Alexa poured a mug of coffee. 'We were happy together,' she said. 'I didn't realise how happy until it was over. I need another mug—I'll go and get one.'

'I'll go. Tell me where they are.'

'In the right-hand cupboard above the sink.' She watched as he casually scooped up the telephone and left her.

They drank their coffee on the deck, looking out over a sea so brilliantly blue that only the surf still lashing the rocks recalled the storm in the night. Luka asked questions about her genealogy software, and she made him smile when she told of her struggles with it and her triumph when eventually she worked out the logic that drove it.

Halfway through her mug of coffee Alexa discovered that she was enjoying herself; although a potent, sexually charged tension still seethed beneath the fragile surface somehow Luka had sidestepped it, and they were talking like—well, like friends.

Don't get excited, she warned herself. Making small talk would be another thing royalty was taught from the cradle.

When the telephone rang, Luka excused himself and answered. Alexa's gaze lingered on the powerful male beauty of his face. Purely as a photographer she admired the strong, angular framework and magnificent colouring of olive and gold and black. Although his handsome face echoed his Mediterranean heritage, the dash of Slav in the cheekbones gave his face a tang of dynamic virility.

She blinked her eyes and dragged her fascinated stare away just in time. After a word that clearly meant the equivalent of goodbye, he said in English, 'The line is down—a lightning strike, by the looks of it. You had better let your friend know.' He handed over the telephone.

Alexa keyed in Sally's number and told her what had happened. 'Bummer for you,' Sally said, clearly in a rush. 'Don't worry about it, Alexa. I'm off to Queenstown in half an hour, but I'll get in touch with Mum and Dad and they can organise it from this end. Thanks a million for letting us know—bye!'

'Bye—have fun skiing!'

Luka held out his hand for the phone.

With a shrug Alexa gave it back, and he said easily, 'You had better come to stay with me until the line is fixed. Apparently it won't take too long.'

That was when she realised that of course he wouldn't let her go back to Auckland; he still didn't trust her not to spill the beans.

Yesterday she'd have scorned his invitation, but yesterday she hadn't sat out on the deck with him, drinking thick, smoky coffee and talking about the complicated tricks software could play. If he'd used that conscious charm on her she'd have told him to go to hell; the Luka who had made her laugh with his lazy wit and humour was very easy to like.

And although he was smiling at her it was with wry understanding, as though he knew how torn she was between indignantly refusing the command hidden in his invitation, and an overweening curiosity.

Because that was all it was. She wanted a peek at his house, and if the price of that was a few hours spent in his company while the power company fixed the line, then she was prepared to pay it. A salty tangle of hair sliding across her cheek decided it for her.

'All right,' she said, adding with a half-smile, 'If I can shower there. A swim is no substitute.'

'Certainly you can.'

Suddenly nervous, she scrambled up. 'I'll get something to change into.'

She had enough self-control not to choose her most flattering outfit, but it was a close-run thing. Alexa packed a few clothes into a small pack and came out to see Luka standing on the deck. Deep inside her some unknown, unsuspected emotion lurched into life, and then slotted into place.

Don't be stupid, she warned herself. You know what he's like—autocratic and high-handed and formidable. And a prince.

As though he'd sensed her approach he turned to meet her, and held out his hand for her bag. 'So,' he said, suddenly very foreign, 'let's go.'

He asked questions about the wildlife while they walked along the beach, describing with humour his surprise the first time he'd seen a family of wallabies eating grass on one of the hillsides.

His gardens extended right down to a wide area of grass beneath the huge pohutukawa trees leaning out across the sand, their roughly barked branches making sweeping statements against the bay. On the way up to the house Alexa noted subtle barriers between the sand and the plantings. As they went through a gate she glimpsed a security camera mounted high to survey the foreshore.

Chilled, she thought angrily that no one should have to live like that. It hadn't even been Luka's choice; he'd been born into the life, with no way out.

She recalled some of the photographs she'd seen of him, many taken with long-range lenses at a time when

he'd thought himself free of surveillance. And years before she'd read an article by one of his lovers, describing
their most intimate moments in salacious detail. A sliver
of resentment dissipated, washed away by compassion.

When, after this holiday, nothing appeared in any
newspaper, perhaps he'd realise that some people could
be trusted.

She smiled up at him, almost staggering at the ferocious response that roared through her when he smiled
back.

He felt it too—fire kindled in the depths of his eyes—
but his expression didn't alter. 'Welcome to my house,'
he said, his voice a little thickened.

Shaken, Alexa forced herself to gaze about with interest as they walked along a wide paved path.

'It's like a series of pavilions,' she said warily, wondering what such a building said about Luka. From a
man of his background she'd expected something luxurious and solidly conventional, harking back to Europe,
but this—this was exotic and fascinating, as beautiful as
the setting.

'It is exactly that,' Luka told her. 'A young Auckland
architect designed it, and did an excellent job.'

'It's stunning.'

Luka escorted her across a wide, partly roofed terrace
overlooking the lush gardens and the sea. Alexa noted
luxurious cane furniture arranged in conversation groups
with a view across the garden.

He took her into the house, tiled with the same tiles
as the terrace, and along a wide hall with glass on both
sides.

Luka opened a door at the far end and said, 'There is
a bedroom you can use.' He gave her another of those
slow, glinting smiles. 'It has a bathroom *en suite.*'

Once inside, bag in hand, the door closed firmly behind her, Alexa let out a soft exhalation of air. Furnished with a simplicity eminently suited to a holiday house, the room was luxurious yet soothing. And it had curtains to cover the windows, so she wasn't exposed to any stray security man, seagull or prince who happened to wander by.

'So relax,' she muttered between clenched teeth as she pushed open a door into a surprisingly large bathroom. Spare and practical, it had been put together with the same unobtrusive opulence and the same attention to detail.

A horrified glance in the mirror revealed a face topped by a bird's nest of copper hair. As she stripped Alexa admitted that, in spite of being an autocratic, infuriating throwback to medieval times, Luka of Dacia had a strictly modern sensibility when it came to interior decoration.

Of course he'd probably just snapped those lean, strong fingers and someone else had done all the work, but was all this understated discretion, this almost aggressive coolness of colour and line, a reaction to growing up in a country with a dark, often bloody, always dramatic history?

He might be an ogre, but he was an interesting man.

And a very clever one. Every woman who saw him sensed a sexy, exciting challenge, because such tightly leashed self-control hinted at passion beyond the usual. And every woman wondered if she'd be the lucky one to unleash it.

Alexa turned away and set the shower going.

'I'll bet no woman ever has. I don't think there's a chance of smashing through his defences,' she murmured. 'I can't even make him lose his temper!'

She suspected that Luka carried his country in his heart's core, a man trained—probably from birth, poor little boy!—to repress everything else to his duty as a ruler.

Although according to the woman who'd sold her story, he'd been a perfect lover: tender, passionate, controlled and—well, generally magnificent.

'So he's great in bed,' Alexa said cynically, walking into the shower with a sigh of relief. Sternly ignoring her half-scared, half-feverish shiver at the thought of him as a lover, she told herself, 'You know that's not everything.'

Damian had been a good lover, and she'd really believed she'd loved him, yet in the end she had left him because she'd loved his large, cheerful, noisy family as much as she'd loved him. More, if she was honest.

And she wanted more than that; she wanted what her parents had had, and her grandmother—a once in a lifetime love.

She wasn't naïve enough to let her fascination with Luka blind her. Sexual attraction was notoriously brittle as a sensible base for any sort of relationship—

'Whoa!' she said out loud, shocked by the thought.

The hand soaping her hair stopped. *Relationship?*

Oh, no. No, no, no! Although no man had affected her as Luka did, she wasn't going to fall into that trap and assume she must be in love with him.

Her unwilling response was solely physical. She felt nothing more for him than anger at his arrogance, respect for his intelligence—and a humiliating surge of hormones.

Without emotion and understanding sex offered no more than a momentary pleasure and a sour aftermath.

Ignoring a stab of pain somewhere in the region of

her heart, she finished washing, dried herself down on an enormous bath sheet and dressed rapidly in the well-cut jeans and a honey-coloured shirt.

She was not going to let herself become obsessed by a man she didn't know and didn't trust. Apart from the huge gulf between a New Zealand woman and a European prince, when this interlude was over he'd go back to Dacia and she'd never see him again. Which, she reminded herself sternly as she gathered up the clothes she'd discarded, would be a good thing; she was far too susceptible to the spectacular charm, which was as much a weapon as his intellect—and used just as ruthlessly.

Someone was in her bedroom when she went back—a thin, middle-aged woman who looked up from straightening cushions on the chair when Alexa stopped in the doorway.

With a hint of reservation, the older woman said, 'Hello, I'm Jill Martin, the housekeeper. If there's anything you want, let me know.'

'Thank you,' Alexa said, smiling.

It wasn't returned. Jill Martin said, 'The Prince asked me to tell you that morning tea will be served by the swimming pool in half an hour.'

CHAPTER SIX

A FEW minutes later, eyes masked with sunglasses, Alexa walked out of the bedroom.

She hadn't taken two steps before the housekeeper reappeared, greeting her with that reserved smile. 'The Prince asked me to show you the way.'

'Thank you.' Alexa walked sedately beside her along the seaward terrace and down some wide steps towards a pale apricot stucco wall, wondering why the woman was so reticent.

Accustomed to making people feel relaxed enough to photograph, she went on, 'This must be a fabulous place to work—a far cry from noisy, busy Auckland.'

'We love it here,' Jill Martin said politely, standing back to let her go through a door in the wall.

Alexa persevered. 'I know it's very new, but the garden looks so established.'

'The landscaper brought in a lot of mature trees, and of course some, like that coral tree, were already here.' The older woman gestured towards a large tree that sheltered a long, low cabana, its claw-like scarlet flowers already bursting free of their buds.

Beyond it a pool glittered under the benign sky. Lounging furniture had been arranged on two sides of the walled enclosure, some in full sun, some in the shade of a pergola, under which Luka was reading. Sprawled along a lounger, he should have looked relaxed and lazy, in spite of the papers he was flicking through, but his big, powerful body radiated leashed purpose beneath the scarlet bouganvillaea cascading above him.

Alexa's gaze flew to his face, strong and angular and harshly compelling. Her breath rasped shallow through her lungs and something splintered in the region of her heart. Every sense was so acutely honed that the cool breeze slashed at her skin and the mellow autumn sunlight flailed it. Even the ironic mew of a gull scraped across her eardrums.

Briefly she closed her eyes, willing herself back into her usual composed self.

Luka glanced up, then got to his feet. Helplessly Alexa noticed the way his T-shirt and trousers tightened across his shoulders and lean hips, calling attention to the length and muscled power of his legs, the balance and co-ordination that combined to forge his masculine grace.

'Thank you, Jill,' he said.

The caretaker's wife smiled at him with real affection before disappearing back to the house.

Luka's voice deepened. 'You look—charming.'

'I—thank you.'

In contrast to the cool courtesy of his words, the sculpted mask of his face remained urbane, almost bland, yet Alexa sensed something relentless and detached behind it. He didn't want her here.

Well, she thought, trying to hide a surprisingly acute twist of pain with brisk common sense, she didn't want to be here either. Yet she didn't entirely blame him for being so suspicious; that third item in the gossip column was pretty damning. If she'd thought he was a member of the pack of photographers who bayed after celebrities like greedy hounds, she wouldn't have wanted *him* anywhere near her.

'Come and have some tea,' he invited.

Alexa poured a cup for herself, and some inky black coffee for him.

Sitting back down in the lounger, he said pleasantly, as one would say to a guest, 'What made you decide to become a photographer?'

'I fell in love with a camera when I was eight.'

'Eight?' His brows rose.

'My father loved photography, and he showed me what to do. The minute I realised I could imprison time with exciting images I was hooked.'

'Imprison time?' he repeated, eyes suddenly keen. 'That's an interesting way to see it—especially as the camera can lie.'

She said, 'A good photographer reveals the truth.'

'Whose—the subject's or the photographer's?'

Alexa hesitated. 'The truth of that moment.'

Although his brows drew together he wasn't exactly frowning. 'I'm sorry you dropped your father's camera.'

'It was just a sentimental thing.' She shrugged. 'Don't worry about it.'

'I will replace it, of course,' he said without expression.

'That won't be necessary. I was the one who dropped it, not you.'

He ignored that to ask, 'Exactly what sort of photography do you do? Portraits? Weddings?'

She'd already told him, but perhaps he was trying to trip her up. Smiling in a way that hinted of teeth, she said, 'Portraits. And some magazine work, even a bit of fashion work—it's all good discipline. Wedding photographers need far more courage and stamina and sheer dedication than I'll ever have. It's like swimming with

tiger sharks—dangerous. Mothers of the bride are no-
torious!'

Entranced by the difference laughter made to his expression, she watched him through her lashes. Nothing
would ever soften his face, but genuine amusement lifted
it beyond gorgeous into blazingly charismatic.

Sobering, he commented drily, 'Not to mention page-
boys and flower girls,' and added, 'Have you noticed
that there is always one child everyone watches with a
mixture of dread and anticipation?'

'Usually the cutest one,' she said, surprised in her turn
by his observation. But then, he was a man who noticed
things.

'Tell me about Dacia,' she suggested, to move the
subject off herself—although she'd developed a curiosity
about the place that had produced a man like Luka. 'I
know it's an island, and very beautiful, and I know it's
had an interesting history, but I'm afraid that's about all
I know.'

Luka wondered why she was bothering, but to keep
his mind—and his body—off the way the sunlight
poured through the flowers onto her vivid, sensuous face,
he said, 'What would you like to know?'

'How is it still a monarchy when every other country
around is a republic?'

'Not every one. Illyria has a prince who married a
New Zealander.'

Alexa nodded. 'We heard about that in spades—the
newspapers called it the romance of the century. Were
you there?'

'Yes. We know each other quite well, Alex Considine
and I.' Another smile hit Alexa with sledgehammer
charm. 'Illyrians consider us a Johnny-come-lately state
because Dacia has been independent only four hundred

or so years, whereas they claim descent from the original Illyria in Roman times. And of course there's Monaco, on the French side of Italy, and a couple of others. We're all accidents of history, and we owe our existence to clever, cunning rulers who were willing to sacrifice almost everything on the altar of their little realms.'

'As your father did,' she said quietly, dark winged brows pleating above her pale, exotic eyes.

He saw the moment she remembered that his mother had been the daughter of the man who'd threatened Dacia with invasion. Colour ran up beneath her silken skin in a manner he found oddly endearing as she looked at him with stricken regret, and his ingrained, carefully constructed suspicion began to crumble.

But only for a second. Her clear, candid gaze invited trust, but Luka remembered a woman who'd looked at him with erotic fervour one night, and the next morning sold every detail of their lovemaking, bargaining with the ruthless skill of a huckster to extract the utmost money from the press.

He'd never spoken of his parents' marriage to anyone, not even his friends. The impulse to tell Alexa how it had been was just another indication of how she'd got to him, like wine laced with poison, he thought fancifully.

Aloud he said neutrally, 'Dacia wasn't big enough to win a war, and when it became obvious that we were on our own my father was forced to temper his actions to the inevitable.' He gave a hard smile. 'He yielded on those things he had to, but within the limits imposed by my grandfather he stood between the people of Dacia and the sort of hell the Illyrians suffered.'

He drained his glass, then set it down. Coolly, without emotion, he said, 'My mother's father was an old-style warlord, but although he kept my father on a tight rein my mother was able to soften a lot of his harsher decrees. She was his only child.'

Alexa felt as though she were walking across fishhooks. 'So the marriage worked out?'

He gave her a brief, oblique smile, but ignored her comment. 'He knew the time for warlords was passing, and I suspect it satisfied something in him to know that one day his grandchild would rule Dacia.'

'Did you like him?' she asked curiously.

His expression didn't change, but she knew she'd intruded across some invisible barrier. 'I didn't know him well,' he said evenly.

Had his father and mother loved each other?

With that unnerving ability to read her mind, Luka drawled, 'Dynastic marriages can be quite satisfactory if both parties understand the rules.'

'And what *are* the rules?' Alexa enquired dulcetly.

'That the couple provide support for each other, and that after producing the required heir—or two—love and excitement may be sought outside the marriage, but always discreetly.' He directed a sardonic smile at her rigid face. 'I can see you don't approve.'

'It sounds remarkably cold-blooded,' Alexa said quietly, gazing out over the glinting water of the pool and feeling profoundly sorry for both his bartered mother and his wily, duty-bound father. And for him, growing up in what must have been a hell of tension.

'So you would demand passion and romance in marriage?' he asked with silky, goading precision.

'Don't most people? As well as respect and liking and companionship, of course.'

'You *are* a romantic,' he said, his voice deep and

taunting. 'Where do you expect to find this paragon of male perfection?'

'I'm not actively looking right now,' she retorted, trying to conceal her bristling hackles.

'And do children enter the equation?' Politely he offered her a plate of delicious little muffins.

Helping herself to one, Alexa said, 'If that's at all possible, yes.'

Although his expression didn't alter his searching scrutiny tightened her skin, and she suspected he understood the source of her deep-seated longing for a family.

Hastily she said, 'For a dynastic marriage to be a success you'd have to be brought up where marriages of convenience are the norm.'

'So you can't see yourself entering into one?'

'Never,' she said crisply. 'But I do think that any relationship should have ground rules, and if both parties agree with them and stick to them the relationship should work.' She added snidely, 'Especially if the expectations are limited. I assume that's the sort of marriage you plan to make?'

He leaned back in his chair and surveyed her with half-closed eyes. 'Probably,' he said indolently, 'unless I find another woman like Ianthe of Illyria, who wears her love for her husband in her face.'

'And does he love her?' Alexa asked, a little more tartly than she'd intended. OK, so she'd given him the opening, but his cold-blooded decision to marry for practical reasons hurt her in some fundamental way.

Luka smiled, all prowling, sexual charm beneath unreadable eyes. 'It's hard to tell. He doesn't give much away.'

'It certainly wasn't a *practical* marriage,' Alexa said before she could stop herself. Ianthe of Illyria, born plain

Ianthe Brown of New Zealand, was a scientist who walked with a limp, a beautiful Cinderella who'd won the heart of her prince.

'Not practical at all,' Luka agreed without inflection.

Something in that level, unemotional voice made Alexa wonder if he even believed in love.

He went on, 'Of course Considine was brought up in Australia after he and his mother fled Illyria. No doubt he absorbed different attitudes and values there.'

Alexa said carefully, 'I hope he and his Ianthe are very happy together.'

Luka's smile had an edge to it. 'Have you ever been in love?'

'Four or five times,' she told him, her cheerful voice ringing hollow even to her own ears. 'How about you?'

His brows rose, but he said evenly, 'A couple of times in my youth, when anything seemed possible.' He glanced across the swimming pool. 'Would you like to swim?'

Another abrupt change of subject. But what did he mean by 'when anything seemed possible'?

Possibly that a man who'd been trained to distrust everyone would never learn to love.

The thought sent icy little needles of pain through her. Such a waste!

'A swim sounds wonderful,' she said sedately, getting to her feet and beginning to stack the dishes on the tray. A swim would also douse the slow, simmering heat permeating her body. 'I'll take this inside and change.'

He accompanied her back to the house, silent beside her while she wondered why on earth she'd agreed to swim. Because he'd challenged her to do it, and she'd responded with a flare of bravado.

If she kept this up she'd be heading into trouble, she

thought on an odd little pang—serious trouble. Although she'd packed her most demure bathing suit, the thought of Luka watching her in it sent sneaky little thrills up her spine.

'The kitchen's through here,' he said, opening the door.

A large room, magnificently set out with every conceivable gadget a cook might lust after, it was empty. Alexa set the tray down on the bench, surprised when Luka began to put the dishes away.

With a swift smile he closed the refrigerator door. 'You see, I'm not entirely without domestic skills.'

She laughed. 'Oh, great skills—putting milk and sugar away and stacking the dishwasher! Can you sort clothes to go into the washing machine?'

'I have tried,' he told her with a vastly different smile, one that set her heart thudding uncomfortably against her breastbone, 'and I've decided that such knowledge is genetically coded into the female of the species.'

'How chauvinist and convenient for you!'

'I'm afraid that goes with the territory.'

The note of warning in his voice chilled Alexa. When he wanted to Luka could be amusing and entertaining, and she enjoyed matching wits with him—enough, in fact, for it to become addictive—but there was always that invisible barrier.

It shouldn't matter, but somehow it did.

If he'd been the seriously sexy, lightweight playboy prince from the headlines, instead of a man with formidable intelligence and uncompromising authority, she wouldn't be feeling this complicated mixture of emotions. The raw sexual attraction, although intensely potent, was probably the easiest to deal with—at least, she thought with a sudden catch of her breath, as long as he didn't touch her.

What frightened her was her growing fascination with the complex and intriguing man beneath that darkly handsome mask.

She looked up sharply when a man walked into the kitchen—the man Luka had sent to bring her to the hotel that day he'd accused her of sending information to the wretched gossip columnist.

Luka frowned, but said pleasantly enough, 'Alexa, you have already met my head of security.'

'I have. Hello,' she said with a smile.

He gave a formal half-bow and said, 'Ms Mytton.'

Luka's voice was cool. 'Dion, what have you discovered about the power to Ms Mytton's house?'

Straightening up, Dion said, 'Not good news, I'm afraid. The line was not brought down by a branch or a tree; it seems that the transformer was struck by lightning.'

'Which means?' Alexa asked.

Luka cut in with smooth reassurance, 'Merely that it will take a little longer to fix. Don't worry about it now—Dion will find out when it will be done. In the meantime, I think we should enjoy that swim.'

Five minutes later, Alexa was wriggling into her periwinkle-blue bathing suit, originally chosen because it lent her eyes some colour. It covered everything, but it was skintight. Normally she'd have worn it quite happily, but—well, this was not a normal occasion.

Trying to ignore the insistent, secret excitement thrumming through her, she pulled her shirt over the suit, then went to the bathroom in search of sunscreen.

She found an unopened bottle—along with other beautifully packaged, untouched cosmetics—in the top drawer. Uncapping the bottle of lotion, Alexa pushed the drawer back in with a quick twist of her hip. A sharp rattle revealed that she must have dislodged something; she pulled the drawer right out to see a tube of lipstick.

Feeling oddly empty, she twisted the lid free. It had been used. Alexa stared at the neatly rounded top as though it were a snake, Sandra Beauchamp's beautiful face flashing into her mind.

'So why the shock?' she said robustly. 'According to the magazines he's not in the habit of holidaying alone!'

She was jumping to conclusions—if Luka had had a woman here, surely she'd shared *his* bed and *his* room?

Perhaps he valued his privacy too much to share a room with a woman.

Recapping the gold case, Alexa set it on the marble counter and with deft, angry movements applied sun-screen to her lips and skin.

Ten minutes later she re-emerged, sunglasses worn as a visor, her face an aloof mask, hoping that Luka wouldn't recognise how absurdly sensitive she felt about the long bare legs emerging beneath the hem of her shirt.

Or see the foolish jealousy seething beneath the glossy surface she'd manufactured.

The housekeeper was walking along the terrace when she emerged into the sunlight. Keeping an eye on her? Before she had time to wonder whether it was sensible, Alexa said, 'Ms Martin, I found a lipstick in a drawer in the bathroom. It's been used, so someone must have left it behind.'

The older woman nodded and said pleasantly, 'I'll deal with it.'

'Thank you.'

Still slightly shaky with a horrible mixture of anger

and jealousy, and a possessiveness she'd never experienced before, Alexa continued on to the pool.

Whoever had designed it had chosen tiles the exact colour of the sea on a sunny day, and organised the water to fall gently over an unseen lip so that the pool and the ocean mingled without an obvious boundary. An infinity edge, and swimming in it would be like floating into space—exhilarating, dangerous, something she'd never done before...

It seemed like a slap in the face when she saw Luka already in the water, striking out fast and purposefully, sunlight gleaming richly on his olive skin.

Watching the sinuous movement of the coiled, powerful muscles in his wide shoulders and long legs, Alexa suffered a spasm of forbidden desire so intense it felt like agony.

Only a few minutes ago she'd been complacently telling herself that she could cope with this elemental response! Instead, she burned in feverish need, every cell in her body aching with a hunger she couldn't control, a hunger that honed the emotions already churning inside her, feeding off their intensity and adding to them.

Like every other woman he met, she'd fallen under Luka's spell. Why else had she just spent half an hour talking to him instead of berating him for treating her like some piece of plunder?

Actually, she decided more reasonably, he'd treated her like an obstacle to neutralise. And now he was swimming as though he'd forgotten her.

Not that she *wanted* him to be interested in her.

Taut with tension, and thoroughly disgusted with herself, Alexa shrugged off her shirt and threw it onto a hammock, tossing her sunglasses onto a low table. After shucking off her sandals, she executed a neat racing dive into the pool well away from Luka.

Cool water sleeked deliciously along her body, but did nothing to douse that treacherous fire inside. Alexa set herself to emulate Luka's determined pursuit of fitness, striking out with her own classic crawl stroke. Well-taught herself, she recognised the signs of an excellent coach, and thought sourly that no doubt he'd had the very best of tuition for anything he desired.

Making love, too. All those impossibly beautiful women who'd shared his bed and his body…

She missed a turn and breathed at the wrong moment. Choking, gasping, she sank to the bottom, pushed off again and shot to the top.

Strong arms snatched her up, lifting her out of the pool. As she lay coughing on the tiles she felt Luka turn her onto her side in the recovery position, holding her there until she stopped spluttering water.

Finally, when she was able to breathe again, she sat up and looked at him with streaming eyes, muttering, 'Th-thanks.'

He was kneeling, his dark face grim with concern. 'Are you all right?' he demanded, tilting her chin so that he could see her face.

'Apart from my wounded pride,' she said with a determined smile. 'I've known since I was three that breathing underwater doesn't work…'

He got to his feet and bent down, his arms closing around her in a tight, warm embrace as he pulled her to her feet. She had to stop herself from curving into him, abandoning herself to his support.

'I thought you were drowning,' he said roughly, picking her up.

He carried her across to the hammock, setting her on

the edge and holding her and the hammock still so that
he could see her properly. 'Can I get you something—
a little brandy, perhaps?'

'No,' she said, trying to stifle another bout of coughing. 'I'm all right. Sorry to interrupt your swim. As soon
as I get my breath back and dredge up some self-esteem,
I'll join you again.'

Arms tightening around her, he started to laugh.

'Truly, I'm fine. You can't drown a water rat,' she
muttered, confused and scared, yet aching with a tense
need that threatened to overturn the warnings thundering
through her mind.

He scanned her face thoroughly. Strident heat stormed
up through her skin, but she met his darkening eyes fear-
lessly.

'Actually, you *can* drown a water rat,' he said with a
strange half-smile, partly cynical, partly aggressive.
'Don't do that again. It scared me.' Almost absently he
lifted his hand to trace the soft outline of her mouth.

Dimly, through the wild hammering of her pulses,
Alexa knew that he might have decided to use the incandescent attraction between them to keep her docile.
At that moment it didn't matter, not when Luka was
looking at her from intent, molten eyes and his fingers
were moving with tantalising lightness against her lips.

Dazzled, bemused, enchanted, she caught one of those
maddening fingers between her teeth and nipped—not
hard, just enough to stop it. He tasted of sun and salt
and water, and a potent male flavour all his own.

As though her bite had been a signal, he tipped her
into the hammock in a tangle of arms and legs, twisting
halfway to land on his back beneath her.

'You've got tiger's eyes,' he said, kissing the hollow
of her throat, where her heart thudded in delicious panic,

'cool and challenging, with an edge of danger, and you've been giving me some very tigerish smiles and glares.'

'What did you expect? You've been behaving like a marauder,' she said, trying to sound as confident as he did.

'Mmm.' He tasted the skin above that fluttering skipping pulse, sending violent jolts of sensation right down to her toes. Laughter gleamed in his tawny eyes. 'I'm not a marauder—just a man with a problem.'

CHAPTER SEVEN

'I CAN feel it,' Alexa muttered, scarlet-faced.

Luka's problem—an urgent, not to say *pressing* problem—was obvious. He was very aroused, and so was she, the hidden places of her body softening and moistening in preparation for his possession.

He gave another heart-shaking smile. 'That,' he said, a touch of lazy ruefulness in his tone, 'is a response, not a problem.'

Alexa opened her mouth, but before she could formulate a tart answer he wound his hands in the tumbled copper hair around her shoulders and kissed the words from her lips.

It was an oddly tender kiss, as was the one that followed, and the one after that—sweet and hungry, yet leashed by his will. Unsatisfied, Alexa lifted her head and opened her eyes, almost flinching away when she saw that hint of laughter still lurking in the gleaming golden depths of his eyes.

For him this was an idle pleasure to fill in a sunny morning—as light and meaningless as the sex he'd presumably had with the woman who owned the lipstick. Whereas what Alexa felt was wild and desperately consuming, raw and real.

She said tightly, 'It might not be a problem for you, but it's one for me.'

Cynicism replaced the amusement in his eyes. He enquired with a mocking smile she disliked, 'Proving a point, Alexa?'

'I don't know—am I?' she asked, scrambling off him. The swaying hammock made it difficult, and as soon as she'd got off it he showed her how it should be done, rising in one swift, lithe movement to tower over her.

'I think so.' This time his smile held an edge of aggression. 'But perhaps I should prove one too...'

Mesmerised, she closed her eyes when the back of his fingers came to rest on the pounding pulse in her throat.

'You remind me of a horse I once had,' he drawled.

Her eyes flew open, snapping with outrage. 'Well, thanks a million!'

'She was a very beautiful mare,' he said, that disturbing mockery edging each word. 'Tall and elegant and fast, with hair the same colour as yours. She refused to allow me to ride her.'

'So what happened to her?' Alexa ground out, pretending to ignore the blatant double meaning. 'Did you have her put down for treason?'

His eyes half closed. 'For a citizen of a modern democratic monarchy, you have a strange idea of how one works,' he said smoothly. 'It's no longer politically correct to chop off people's heads just because they disagree with you. No, I broke her to my will. It didn't take me long to have her eating out of my hand and allowing me to ride her whenever I chose.'

Pagan heat raced through Alexa's body. Defying it, she lifted her brows and said with a cheesy smile, 'How very masterful of you.'

He smiled, increasing his grip on her shoulders and drawing her towards him. The knowledge that she wanted him to kiss her rather more than she wanted to take her next breath should have terrified Alexa, but she didn't resist.

'Of course I had to gentle her first,' he said, and released one shoulder to lift her chin. 'It wasn't easy because she was flighty and suspicious and hot-tempered—a challenge I couldn't resist.'

His touch seared through Alexa's crumbling defences like a sword slashing silk. Her skipping, pounding heart echoed through her brain, drowning her thoughts in a ferocious physical response.

'Did I say she was beautiful enough to ravish a man's heart from his breast?' he asked in an abrasively sensual voice. 'Sleek and strong and glorious, like wind over the ocean, like the sun in its glory, like a tigress defending her young...'

And he kissed her, moulding her against him. For long moments they stayed locked together, until he made an odd harsh sound in his throat and deepened the kiss, and she responded with an excitement that flared into a conflagration.

Lost in the incandescent world of the senses, Alexa slid her arms up and around his neck, offering herself to his mouth, to his hands. Luka accepted that mute invitation, making himself master of her mouth as his fingers cupped the swelling mound of her breast, touching it with sure knowledge of how to please her.

Mindless, intense and perilous, wildfire blasted through her, sizzling from her mouth and her breast to the source of all pleasure in the pit of her stomach.

And then he lifted his head to smile into her dazed face with its heavy-lidded eyes and pleading mouth.

His golden eyes darkened. With a muttered oath he released her and stepped back.

Almost gulping air into her panicking lungs Alexa stared around, slowly realising where she was as memory came crashing back, accusing her of stupidity and shaming surrender.

She stumbled back, humiliated to the soles of her feet. 'How the hell do you *do* that?' she whispered, inwardly raging and bereft.

All emotion vanished from his eyes, leaving them flat and metallic. 'There's no magic spell,' he said in a voice that sliced what little composure she had left into shreds. 'You are a beautiful woman and I am a healthy man with the usual appetites.'

'I'm not talking about my effect on you,' she snarled, her twisting hands belying her tone. 'Most men are easily—' She bit back the scathing words.

His wide shoulders lifted in a shrug. 'Women are not so different from men,' he said carelessly. 'And don't try to convince me that this hasn't happened to you before—you knew what you were doing.'

At least she'd kept something of herself hidden from him. This overwhelming physical attraction was completely new and alien.

'Never without emotion,' she returned, swivelling away with his kisses still burning her lips and his touch setting every secret place in her body alight with a forbidden anticipation. 'I'm going.'

'The night we met,' he said, his thoughtful voice stopping her, 'you looked at me with a kind of shocked, defiant resistance. I recognised it because that's how I was feeling too—as though I'd been ambushed by a challenge both intoxicating and dangerous.'

His hand moved with sure delicacy to the sensitive place where her neck met her shoulder, leaving a trail of fire. Alexa shivered, and he laughed again. The next moment she was in his arms, shuddering with pleasure as he kissed the pulsating hollow in her throat.

The thin wet material of her bathing suit might just as well not have existed. When he closed his lips around the incredibly sensitive point of her breast a spasm of intolerable excitement twisted through her, banishing all thought; unable to control her response, she arched into him.

'*That* is the problem,' he said in a thick, impeded voice, straightening abruptly and picking her up. 'Breathe in.'

Aching with frustration, she dragged air into her lungs. Luka took the three steps across to the pool as though she weighed nothing, stepping off the edge with her still locked in his arms.

Cool and bracing, the water closed around them. He kissed her again, hard and heated, and then released her, pushing her upwards in a swirl of water.

Opening her eyes when she broke the surface, Alexa saw the muscles across his back bunch as he hauled himself out of the pool. She sank back beneath the water and turned to swim for the other side, pulses jumping like a jackhammer.

He was waiting, hand outstretched. Reluctantly, still in an anguish of frustration, she accepted his help and was drawn free of the pool.

'Come for a walk with me,' he said, enough command in his tone to ensure she knew it was deliberate.

'Do I have a choice?'

His eyes mocked her. 'Of course you have a choice.'

'As long as I do what you want!'

'If that were so,' he said, challenging eyes boring into her as he pushed back a lock of hair clinging to her cheek, 'you'd be lying under me in the hammock right now.'

Flushing, she jerked her hand away and almost ran to collect her shirt, her skin burning more deeply as she saw the creases pressed into it by the combined weight of their bodies. She shrugged into it, using it as a shield against his hard, perceptive gaze.

'Is that how constitutional monarchs normally behave? I thought you were brought up to duty and service and self-sacrifice?' she scoffed, casting a derisive glance at the pool and the luxurious furniture.

'Oh, I enjoy the trappings,' he said deliberately, his eyes hardening, 'but that's all they are—trappings.'

'Like sex?' Angry because she passionately wanted to be more to him than a playmate for an afternoon, she added curtly, 'Sorry, but I'm not a trapping.'

With a narrow, knife-edged smile Luka gestured towards the garden. 'Neither is sex.'

End of discussion, she thought grimly. She certainly wasn't going to continue on that subject!

The grounds had been skilfully and superbly landscaped, but Alexa noted that the walls were high enough to deter any but the most determined intruder, and discreet surveillance cameras were dotted here and there.

'I hope there isn't a camera in the pool area,' she said, her skin heating again.

He ignored her question to say blandly, 'The cameras are turned off when I'm in the garden.'

'I don't want to star in a pornographic movie,' she snapped, sure now that he spent long hours seducing women by the pool. She glared up at him. 'In fact, I want to see the films from these cameras.'

He gave a crack of wry laughter. '*Touché*. Relax—you'd find them incredibly boring.'

'Just as you'll find my negatives,' she said grimly.

Brows slightly raised, he looked at her for a long moment before smiling faintly. 'Perhaps,' he conceded.

Alexa swallowed, swiftly looking away in search of something to comment on. 'Oh,' she said gratefully, her voice suddenly soft, 'a cotton rose! My grandmother used to have one in her garden.'

Luka said, 'A cotton rose? I thought it was a double hibiscus.'

'It does look like a hibiscus, doesn't it? But the flowers last longer—at least three days.'

He nodded. 'And change colour each day.'

'They fascinated me when I was a kid—opening white, then turning that pretty rose colour and ending up this lovely dark pink.' She touched one with a caressing finger. 'Why do you need all this security?'

'You should know.' His voice was brusque. 'The night we met you were almost attacked.'

With a final glance at the cotton roses, Alexa moved on. 'That was in the city. No one knows you're here, and even if they did they wouldn't intrude. You might get a few wallaby hunters trespassing, although you could just send a minion out to warn them off.'

He laced her fingers through his. 'I can cope with those hunting four-legged prey.'

Fighting back a scorching pleasure, it took her a moment to comprehend what he meant. Appalled, she glanced up, to meet eyes as smooth and opaque as the metal they resembled. 'But this is New Zealand—we don't go in for assassinations or kidnapping!'

'It can happen anywhere,' he said, his tone suddenly harsh.

Alexa glanced up, but with a face and voice that revealed nothing, he went on, 'This is to keep the press out. And, yes, possibly I'm paranoid, but your profession is extremely determined and cunning when it comes to stalking prey.'

'I am not a press photographer,' she said between her teeth. 'I can imagine how frustrating it must be to be dogged by paparazzi, but have you ever thought that the publicity has been good for you and Dacia?'

His eyes gleamed beneath his thick lashes. Derisively he asked, 'In what way, apart from giving me an edge when it comes to business negotiations?' He answered her enquiring look with a narrow, humourless smile. 'No one expects a pin-up, playboy prince to be any good at anything more serious than skiing,' he explained.

'So they underestimated you.' She nodded wryly, knowing how the anonymous 'they' felt, because she too had taken him at surface value. 'Oh,' she said in an entirely different tone, 'who is this?'

An elderly Labrador came sniffing around the palm tree. Obviously sure of its welcome, it advanced, tail wagging in ingratiating enthusiasm. Alexa stooped and stroked its blonde head, smiling as it sighed and leaned against her knee.

'Good girl,' Alexa said, fondling the dog's soft ears, then looked up to ask with a hint of disapproval, 'Is she yours?

'No, she belongs to the caretaker and his wife.' He surveyed her with a glimmering, tawny gaze. 'Don't you think I should have a dog?'

'Dogs are social animals. They need companionship, not jet-setting owners.'

'So we agree on something,' he said ironically.

Straightening up, Alexa said, 'If you're so worried about paparazzi storming your compound, I'd have thought you'd have several Dobermanns or German Shepherds at the ready, not one darling old Lab.'

He said evenly, 'There are others around,' and bent to stroke the Lab.

Something compressed into yearning deep inside Alexa as she noted the way sunlight gleamed blue-black on his head when he bent to stroke the pleading dog. Hardly breathing, she traced the bold caress of the sun on the dense lashes that hid his brilliant eyes, on the chiselled perfection of his mouth as he murmured to the dog.

She tore her gaze away and fixed it on a tree she'd never recognise again. From behind she heard him say, 'I envy you—and old Bonny here—your serene conviction that the world is a benign place.'

'No, you don't. You think we're totally naïve,' she said quietly, setting off between banks of shrubs and flowers with the dog snuffling along behind. Compelled to discover more about him, she asked, 'Surely you trust—or trusted—someone. Your family? Your chief bodyguard?'

His broad shoulders lifted and fell in a negligent shrug. 'If you can't trust your family, who can you trust? And Dion is not a bodyguard—he's a security expert.'

The one who organised all these lights and cameras, no doubt.

Alexa recognised the evasion, but the words she'd been about to say dried on her tongue. Luka was smiling down at her, using his magnetic charm to veil a keen scrutiny.

This jaunt through the garden was a warning. He wanted her to know she didn't have a chance of sneaking into his house without being caught and humiliatingly exposed.

She was angry and hurt, yet the reluctant, uncontrollable excitement surging through her summoned an answering smile, one she strove to control.

Luka noticed the telltale steady stare, the limpid, practised movement of her full, lush mouth, and wondered cynically why he was disappointed. With himself, per-

haps, because he had to fight down a stupid desire to
trust her.

After hearing from Dion—who'd searched the bach
and discovered no more cameras—that she'd told him
the truth, Luka had even found himself concocting scenarios that might explain those three tell-tale items in
the gossip column, when he knew the most logical reason was almost certainly the right one. She had sold
them to the columnist.

There had been no more since he'd silenced her by
removing her camera and mobile phone.

For a second he toyed with the idea of how things
could have been between them, but discarded the fantasy
before it had time to lodge in his brain. He'd been
brought up to believe that duty was paramount, and he
couldn't change now.

He had to keep his hands off her, even though the
temptation to take what she offered with such reluctant
ardour ate into him like a sweetly corrosive acid, filling
his dreams with passion and his brain with sensual
smoke.

Guy's welfare was far more important than slaking
this urgent desire to strip her naked and take her, sink
into the lithe lushness of her body and watch her con-
vulse with shattering pleasure in his arms.

Once an accord between the rebels and the government had been signed, and peace-keeping forces had
moved into Sant'Rosa, Guy's value as a hostage would
disappear and it wouldn't matter how many columnists
Alexa contacted or what she reported about him or his
whereabouts. In the meantime, he needed to keep a low
profile from the press; nothing must leak about a possible peace process or his involvement. He'd have to

keep Alexa an unwitting prisoner, making sure she didn't leave the island or communicate with anyone else.

And the easiest way was to keep her here, where he could supervise her.

He said thoughtfully, 'I am not happy at the thought of you staying down there with no electricity.'

Those astonishing eyes splintered into ice crystals. 'I can manage,' she told him.

No doubt about that, he thought; she was surprisingly practical. 'No water, no cooking—'

'There's the barbecue,' she pointed out, square chin angling up as it always did when she crossed swords with him, 'and if someone could get the hatch off the tank I could dip water out.'

'Why not spend the night here? The power should be back on tomorrow.'

Looking down at the dog, she turned her face half away. Luka was accustomed to the untamed charge of sexual desire at the sight of a beautiful woman, but something about the straight line of Alexa's nose and the proud, sensuous curve of her mouth, the angle of her chin as it jutted slightly, punched him in the heart. It was a weakness he couldn't afford.

He said coolly, 'I won't touch you again.'

Colour smoked across her cheekbones and her mouth bloomed. Relief? He didn't think so. But although she was tempted, she wasn't going to give in. He said with a smile, 'Admit that you'll be more comfortable here.'

Alexa knew she should go back to the bach. She was dicing with danger staying here, talking to him, watching him, wondering about him. 'I'm surprised. Does this mean that you trust me not to go bleating to the nearest newspaper as soon as I get back to Auckland about my

"Secret Tryst with the Prince of Dacia"?' she said
tartly.

He laughed. 'It won't matter if you do. I'll have had
my peaceful holiday, and I'm accustomed to opportunist
lies. Besides, I don't think that's your style.'

'But selling titbits of information to a gossip columnist is?' she flashed, hiding her chagrin and hurt with a
slicing anger.

'The jury's out on that one,' he said softly, eyes lanc-
ing across her face. He smiled. 'If you stay I can promise
you a much better dinner than anything you could con-
coct on that wreck of a barbecue. And a decent shower.'

The suggestion of trust cut her resistance into shreds.
'Appealing to my stomach is a low blow,' she said, anticipation fizzing through her. 'Thank you, I'd like to
stay the night here. But I'll need some things from the
bach.'

'We can walk along—or I'll send Jill down to pack
up your clothes,' he said.

'I'll get them,' Alexa said immediately.

'I'll come with you.'

She started to protest, but stopped. Beneath that pleasant, lightly amused façade she sensed cold determination. 'All right,' she said with a shrug.

Before she went to bed Alexa stared at her reflection
with acute foreboding. She'd spent the evening trying
very hard to keep her head while Luka dazzled her with
sophisticated charm and intelligent, interesting conversation. Her eyes were heavy-lidded and slumbrous, her
mouth somehow softer and more curved—asking for
kisses, she thought hollowly.

'You should have said no. Tomorrow, power or not,
you're going back to the bach,' she told that betraying

reflection. 'You only managed to hang onto your wits by a thread tonight.'

The next morning found her edgy and thoroughly unsettled, her defences crumbling more every time Luka smiled at her.

Which he did frequently. She could have resisted the smiles, but the conversation that accompanied them was fascinating and intensely stimulating.

Like the man himself—and not just physically, she told herself crossly, turning again at the end of the pool and forcing her weary arms and legs to propel her through the water. It wasn't fair that a man with such blazing physical charisma should also give her brain such a workout. And he treated her opinions with respect, which was very seductive.

Luka strolled across to the edge of the pool and observed, 'Time to come out.'

Tempted to ignore him, she floated to a stop. 'Why?' she asked belligerently, squinting up at the tall outline haloed by the sun.

'Because you're tiring.' His voice warmed on a hidden note of amusement. 'Do you want me to come in and help you?'

Sensation zinged through her. 'You don't have to,' she said loftily, and swam over to the steps.

His smile widened a little, leaving her with the uncomfortable suspicion that he understood too much of what was going on in her head.

And her body.

He tossed her a towel. 'Thanks,' she said, and dried herself down before walking across to the shaded area. Her legs felt heavy and she had to stop herself from collapsing into the cushioned lounger. She'd been an

idiot to swim so long, but she'd needed to work off the
restlessness prowling through her body.

'Sunscreen,' Luka said, offering her a bottle.

'Thank you,' she said again, more formally this time,
and sat down to apply it to her arms and legs and shoulders, recklessly aware of his smouldering gaze as she
deliberately smoothed her hands across her skin.

In a cool voice he said, 'I hope you don't make a
habit of wearing yourself out in the water. It's dangerous.'

'I'm very careful when I swim alone,' she returned
briskly.

His dark brows met in a frown as he settled back into
his lounger. Good; at least she wasn't the only one affected by this rash impulse to flirt with disaster. Lying
in the sun usually drained her of energy; she applied
herself to caging the feverish desire twisting inside her.

It didn't work. In spite of liberal doses of common
sense and self-derision, that disturbing, perilous hunger,
compelling and merciless, simmered like a hidden volcano through every cell in her body. Rolling over, she
murmured, 'It's too hot here! I'll go up and change. And
then I'd better go back to the bach.'

'I'll see if the electricity is on again,' Luka decided,
getting to his feet.

A woman who enjoyed solitude, she'd normally have
found his constant presence irritating. It was a measure
of her infatuation that she liked it, she thought despairingly as they went back to the house.

A long, cold shower did nothing to ease the fever in
her blood. She put on a fine cotton shirt and a pair of
slender cinnamon pants, combed her hair back from her
face, and folded her clothes and toiletries into her pack

before settling down in one of the chairs out on the covered deck. From inside she could hear Luka's voice.

Wired and restless, she tried to concentrate on the lush fertility of the garden below, backed by the ocean spread in peacock-blue glory to the misty line where it met the sky.

Almost immediately Luka joined her, darkly dominating the vista before her with his forceful presence. 'They haven't changed the transformer yet,' he told her, 'so there's still no power.'

She frowned. 'Nevertheless, I'll have to go.'

He sat down, putting a folder of papers on the table beside his chair. 'Stay for lunch,' he said easily.

Alexa opened her mouth to refuse, but he smiled at her and the words dried on her tongue. What harm could it do? some traitor in her brain asked. He'd go soon, and she'd never see him again; he'd stop being Luka, infuriating, fascinating, utterly absorbing, and become the Prince of Dacia, a handsome mask in the media.

'Thank you,' she said recklessly.

After lunch he defused her turbulent craving by suggesting a ride; she agreed.

Mounted on a pleasant, easy-riding mare befitting her status as a horsewoman, she tried to forget his suggestive story about the other mare while admiring his effortless control of a much larger gelding. Since his promise yesterday not to touch her again, he'd been charming but impersonal, and it was ridiculous and masochistic to miss the elemental undercurrent of awareness.

By the time they got back to the house it was late afternoon and Alexa said firmly, 'Whether the power is on or not, I'll go back to the bach now.'

'I'll check,' Luka said. He rang on the house telephone, and frowned at the reply he got to his question.

'Not yet,' he said, putting the receiver down. 'Jill rang half an hour ago to see what was happening, and they said they'll be replacing the transformer tomorrow.' He said coolly, 'You might as well stay another night, Alexa.'

Alexa bit her lip. If he'd tried to pressure her she'd have left, but it did seem silly to go back to the bach with its inconveniences when she could stay here.

And she really wasn't in any danger. It wasn't as though she was falling in love with the man! OK, she was fascinated, both physically and mentally, but that would soon wear off once he went back to his world.

One last night, and then she'd leave—and just to make sure she didn't cross that invisible line between infatuation and something more dangerous she'd go straight back to Auckland. Oh, she wouldn't tell Luka; if he still believed she was in contact with that wretched gossip columnist he'd probably try to stop her going.

Perhaps when nothing appeared in the newspapers he'd realise that he could trust one woman at least. 'Thank you,' she said. She looked down at her clothes and sniffed delicately. '*Eau de* horse and seawater,' she said. 'I'll go and change.'

Because it would be her last night she chose a soft paisley shirt in shades of gold and copper and ice blue overlong trousers, and drew her hair back from her face in a sleek knot.

'I thought we'd eat by the pool,' Luka said lazily after a swift, appreciative appraisal. He'd changed clothes too, a slim-fitting black shirt and trousers transforming him into some dangerous paladin from a more barbaric past age. 'It's going to be a magnificent sunset.'

It was, staining the sky in a gaudy rage of scarlet and crimson and gold that faded into softer pastels as day was overtaken by night. Someone had lit the large torch flares; in the rapid darkness their light flickered on Luka's tanned, angular face, intensifying the burnished gold of his eyes, the slashing cheekbones and the disciplined, strongly marked mouth.

Little rills of lightning ran through Alexa, sparking fire wherever they touched. Luka was far from the indolent playboy she'd assumed him to be, coasting through life on his charm and his rank. His dry sense of humour entertained her, and she knew now that he liked blue vein cheese, and the sort of classical music she felt needed a good tune, that he found opera entertaining but the emotions too obvious and stereotyped, that he liked Botticelli and Picasso....

Oh, she knew far too much about him! In fact, over dinner, she began to suspect she could spend the rest of her life discovering things about him.

But of course she wasn't in love with him!

'Some liqueur with your coffee?' he asked when the meal was finished.

'No, thank you.' Although she'd drunk very sparingly of the excellent wine, her head was fogged by emotions she had no right to indulge.

'You're shivering,' he said, frowning.

'I'm just a little chilly,' she lied. 'I should go in, I think.' She tried to smile, but her stiff mouth moved awkwardly. 'In fact, I should go home.'

For the space of a heartbeat he stayed immobile, the tough, uncompromising bone structure that gave his face its strength and authority standing out in stark relief. A stray breeze tossed light from the flares high into the air so that it fell across him.

Alexa's heart stopped. He looked like a buccaneer, dangerous and grim and ruthless.

Then, as though compelled by something even more powerful than his steely string of will, he pulled her into his arms and held her against the thudding of his heart, in the perilous heat of his embrace.

If his reluctance hadn't been so clear she might have resisted him, but the realisation that he couldn't resist her was headier than any wine, more alluring than lazy, sweet-tongued temptation itself. As though she had found the home she'd been searching for, she relaxed against him.

An ancient instinct hissed a warning.

Suddenly afraid of her own weakness, she lifted her face to meet his hooded eyes, and said in a hoarse, abrupt voice, 'This is a bad idea.'

'For once, I don't care. You've been driving me insane ever since we met, and I know it's been the same for you. Kissing you is like capturing a piece of heaven.' His glittering survey dragged her soul from her body, until he bent his head and kissed her with concentrated hunger.

Alexa's expectant body sprang into eager life. Within a charged, primal moment she was giving him back kiss for kiss, knowing where this would end and not caring that it would lead nowhere.

'Alexa?' he said against her mouth, giving her the choice.

She sighed into his mouth. 'Yes.'

He lifted her and carried her across to the hammock. Lit only by stars and the dying torches, drugged by desire, she forgot yesterday, forgot everything, and pulled him down with her as she went up in flames.

He wooed her with potent kisses, gentling her with caresses that smoothly banished the last of her fears, so that she slid her hand into the opening of his shirt, seeking a way to the sleek, muscular body beneath. He laughed under his breath and lay back beside her, wordlessly giving her access to him.

Alexa lifted herself, adjusting herself to the sway of the hammock. Carefully, watching the play of her fingers against the dark fabric of his shirt, she began to undo the buttons.

His chest rose and fell abruptly. Alexa's hand froze as she realised that he was holding back, deliberately controlling his hunger; she wanted him to be lost to the same frightening passion that gripped her.

She stared at him with a narrowed, intent look, pale eyes smouldering between their black lashes. The amusement fled from his expression and a much more primitive reaction took its place.

'Do you know what you're doing?' he asked, his voice a low growl that sent anticipatory shivers along her nerves.

'Yes.' *Yes*, she thought, smitten by a savage pleasure. He was still resisting her, but now she understood her own power; she could breach the barriers of his iron determination.

CHAPTER EIGHT

SLOWLY Alexa lowered her head. As though some other, much more experienced woman possessed her, she flicked her tongue along Luka's beautiful mouth. He lay very still, big body taut, eyes fiercely turbulent.

Then she kissed him, nuzzling his mouth open and losing herself in the deep carnality of it.

Luka's arms contracted around her, hauling her down against his lean length while the hammock rocked beneath them. Their bodies flowed together, and Alexa wanted him so much the need ate at her like a hot tide—merciless, overwhelming, and perilously exciting.

Sighing, she surrendered to the dark enchantment, going willingly when he eased her over onto her back and bent his head to her throat and her shoulders.

He had to know that her breasts were heavy and taut and eager, that his least touch through her shirt sent agonised anticipation sizzling through her. By the time he reached that acutely sensitive skin with kisses she didn't protest when he stripped off her shirt and bra.

The cool evening air breathed against her, tightening her nipples. Shivering, she lifted dazzled eyes and searched his face, each angle and plane more harshly etched than usual.

Some faint recollection of where she was penetrated far enough for her to mutter, 'Someone might come.'

Indolently, skilfully, he shaped her soft curves. Electricity sparked from his fingers, from the erotic heat of his mouth on her breast, from the sensuous contrast of dark skin against pale, male strength against feminine softness.

'One of the few advantages of being who I am,' he said raggedly, 'is that no one will come unless I call them.'

The words were kisses against her breasts, the silken rasp of his cheeks an exquisite friction that dispatched more white-hot sensation through her, swift and sure as wine into every cell of her body. Lifting heavy lashes, Alexa drowned in his gaze.

Struggling to think, she asked, 'Do you have any protection?'

Surprise clamped his mouth into a straight line, but almost immediately it relaxed. 'Yes.'

Alexa closed her eyes.

Just this once she'd forget everything but this, she thought, tempted beyond bearing by the incandescent pleasure that sang in her heart, melting her last inhibition. She'd thought she knew something about sex, but Luka was teaching her how innocent she was in all the ways that mattered.

Running her tongue along her dry lips, she forced up her weighted eyelids, making herself scan his hard, intent face.

He wasn't going to persuade her. She'd never be able to believe he'd swept her off her feet—she was co-operating in her own seduction. What would it be like for him to lose that iron armour of self-possession? She suspected that no woman knew, and wondered if...

No. That way would lie disillusion. Emotions weren't trustworthy; they messed things up.

Let it be honest—a straightforward slaking of the powerful, untamed need that had sprung into sinful life the first time their eyes had met.

Responding mindlessly to the skilled tenderness of his hand on her skin, her body made the final decision for her, suddenly racked with a tension that could only be eased by arching up into him and pressing herself against his lean hardness.

Instantly, before she could pull away, his arms clamped around her and he held her stretched beneath him.

The elemental heat and pressure of his body against hers, the faint mingled scent of salty air, flowers and aroused male, set the tinder to her desire. Shuddering, she made an odd noise, half-groan, half-purr, then turned her head into his throat and used the edge of her teeth in a series of punishing little kisses along it.

His body flexed against hers, but his control held. 'Slowly,' he said in a thick, abrasive tone. 'This is not a time for haste.'

He bent his head and kissed the circle of rosy flesh at the centre of her breast, lightly, teasingly, as the nipple puckered and stood proud. An intolerable need for something more made her twist restlessly, but apart from the quickening heat of his body he ignored her silent plea and eased her trousers downwards, exposing her navel to his gaze.

His understanding of just what she craved, what gave her the most pleasure, proclaimed a vast experience of women. Alexa drove that thought to the back of her mind.

Her skin tightened as his mouth explored each breast, worshipping it with kisses, tormenting her with tiny tastes until she groaned and held his head there, fingers sinking into his black hair while she wordlessly demanded that he give her what her body had been longing for.

The tantalising pressure of his mouth increased, became ravenous, and she cried out as exquisite urgency flooded through her, replaced too soon by a dark and demanding hunger.

Her hands came up to grasp his lean hips and bring him over her. He moved, but although the pressure and rhythmic thrusting of his loins against her most sensitive part dazzled her almost to delirium, it wasn't enough. It hurt not to open herself to him, take him and enfold him and hold him in her—make him hers for a few precious minutes.

'Will this be enough for you?' he demanded.

'No,' she said harshly. 'I want you.'

He stripped her trousers away, then lay back; arms folded behind his head, eyes gleaming beneath their thick fringe of lashes, he invited, 'Take me, Alexa.'

Flushed, her body afire, she eased his clothes over his hips, fascinated by the fullness of his penis as she tried to free it from the prison of cloth.

He wasn't in the least shy; why on earth was she so fumble-fingered?

Abruptly he caught her hands and pulled them away. Shocked and humiliated, she looked up into a drawn, stark face.

Luka said harshly, 'I'm not going to last if you keep doing that,' and divested himself of his remaining clothes.

She'd expected a swift possession, but he lay looking at her as she came down beside him, his mouth compressed and his eyes narrowed. Skin puckering in a cool breeze, she met his gaze steadily.

'Sure?' he asked quietly.

'Very sure.'

He smiled and leaned over and began to explore her navel with his tongue.

Shocked, she lay rigid, until the erotic little caress stirred her senses into full clamour, storming through her with the force of an explosion.

Against the soft curve of her stomach he murmured, 'You are so beautiful—sleek and strong as silk...'

'You're beautiful too,' she said wistfully.

'But you don't like touching me?'

Startled, she protested, 'I do.'

'Then why aren't you?'

Shyly she lifted her hand and flexed her fingers against his chest, following with her hand the pattern of hair before sliding her arms around him. Drowning in touch, she learned with her palms and fingertips the taut, coiled contours of the muscles beneath his sleek, hot skin.

She kissed his shoulders, nipped along the powerful breadth with tiny bites, moving with languorous deliberation.

Until eventually he rasped, 'That's enough,' and pulled her hips into his. 'Look at me,' he commanded.

Alexa's lashes fluttered up, meeting eyes that seared into her soul.

'Say my name,' he said, easing slowly into her.

She summoned enough air to breathe. 'Luka.'

'Alexa,' he said, claiming her, and thrust home, powerful shoulders bunching as he took possession.

It hurt a little, but no small pain could prevent the pleasure that assailed Alexa. Gasping, she met the full force of his body with her own strength, gripping him tightly inside her as he pulled back, only to repeat the same voluptuous process until an unknown anticipation drove her to silently demand more than this calculated seduction.

Yet still he remained in full control, using his body as an instrument to summon pleasure, building that pleasure so slowly she could have screamed with the ravishing torture. The world narrowed down to this knife-edge of rapture, keen and savagely consuming. As Luka played her like a master musician a primal force gathered deep in the pit of her stomach, taking over her body until she soared past the limit it could bear.

Hurled into a climax so intense it almost tore her apart, she gasped his name and surrendered to ecstasy. When she could think again above the sound of her heart juddering in her chest and her breathing, she lay in his arms and wondered why of all men it should be Luka...

Always before she'd wondered whether that was all there was to it. This time she thought dazedly that any more and she'd have died. The human body wasn't built to take so much ecstasy.

But she'd been alone on that pinnacle of sensual abandon; Luka hadn't reached his peak.

She opened heavy eyelids and saw him smile. 'All right?' he asked quietly.

He knew, of course, that this had never happened to her before. For a second she almost hated him—until he bent his head and kissed a certain spot beneath her ear. Astoundingly her body responded with renewed desire as with devilish talent he coaxed the afterglow until it leapt from satiation to a sharp hunger and she called out his name in appeal.

'Soon,' he said, growling the word. 'Soon now.'

And this time it was even better, lasted longer, causing an agony of rapture as he drove towards his peak. Out of control now, Luka thrust deep and hard, and beneath him and around him Alexa convulsed and cried out, wrenched from the foundations of her world, reborn into a new one. Everything she knew about herself vanished, leaving her like an amnesiac, alone and frightened in a hostile, unknown world.

'Hush, *cara*, it's all right,' Luka said eventually in a deep quiet voice, turning onto his back. He pulled her into the comforting prison of his arms and swept back her tangled, damp hair to kiss her forehead with the sort of tenderness he'd probably give a child. 'Do you always cry, or have I hurt you?'

Alexa couldn't tell him. It was painfully clear that he felt nothing like her enormous desire to give and give and give until she had nothing left to give. Although he'd enjoyed making love to her, for him it was simply sex.

Whereas for the rest of her life she'd remember the man who'd transported her into this transcendental ecstasy. Even worse, she'd measure every other man by him.

Listening to the joined thunder of their hearts, Alexa smiled, a bittersweet smile as old as time, the smile of a woman who lies in the arms of the lover she knows won't stay.

'Alexa?'

'You didn't hurt me,' she mumbled.

'Sure?'

'Positive.'

Luka picked up a tress of hair and curled it around her shoulder like a veil of copper silk. 'Where did such warm Mediterranean colouring come from?' he asked idly.

'My father was half-Italian.'

He ran a gentle finger along the inside of her arm,

sending explicit shivers along her waiting nerves. 'And your mother was Scandinavian?'

'Scandinavian? No, she was English—well, her ancestors came from Cornwall, actually. What made you think she was Scandinavian?' Alexa asked drowsily, grasping a meagre contentment in lying like this against him and talking.

'Pale eyes like yours come normally from the northernmost parts of Europe.'

Alexa said dreamily, 'I got those from my father too. Just about the only thing I inherited from my mother was her red hair.'

He kissed a spot on her shoulder, letting his lips linger there. Alexa ran her fingers through his hair, revelling in the simple pleasure it gave her to touch him like this—tenderly, with the ravenous sexuality temporarily sated. And underlying that physical satisfaction was a deeper, more emotional contentment, because making love must mean he'd learned to trust her. A little, anyway, she amended—enough to believe that she wouldn't sell salacious details of his prowess as a lover to the media.

'So your Italian father had those amazing eyes?' he asked, each word another kiss against her skin.

'Yes,' she said bemusedly. 'And according to my grandmother he inherited them from his father.'

'Did your grandfather die young?'

Alexa paused. Once she'd told him she'd be saying goodbye for ever to any wispy, romantic hope of a happy ending. Even if Luka no longer suspected her to be a member of the paparazzi, princes made only the most basic of commitments to the children of bastards. Mistress or lover, yes, but forget anything else, anything permanent.

Well, so be it. This was a relationship destined to go nowhere. He was a prince and she was a nobody; he planned a convenient marriage with a woman who'd accept the constraints of such a union—status and sex in return for children. Alexa wouldn't settle for anything less than love.

She wasn't ashamed of her family, and that barely-formed hope was a stupid delusion!

'He died before my father was born,' she said evenly. 'My grandmother went to Italy to study the language at university and met him there—he was a student too. They fell in love, but when he died she came back to New Zealand and raised his son here. All we have of him is a photograph someone took of them both.' She said defensively, 'You can tell they loved each other very much, and my grandmother never looked at another man.'

'When were they together?'

A little surprised—and pleased—at his interest, she told him.

'What was his full name?'

Alexa shrugged. 'My grandmother never told anyone.'

Casually he asked, 'How do you feel about that?'

She hesitated before admitting, 'It's like having a hole in your life. I'm not obsessive, but it would be—well, it would be nice to know that I'm not entirely alone in the world, that there's someone else who has eyes like mine, someone who might remember what my grandfather was like.' She shrugged a little uncomfortably. 'I've tried contacting the university, but got nowhere. Mind you, I suppose a handsome grey-eyed Italian didn't give them much to go on! And any Italian family would probably disown me, as the one thing I do know is that they weren't married.'

'Italians have moved with the times,' Luka told her drily, although he seemed to be thinking of something else. 'What do you know about your grandfather?'

'I know that my father was called Nicholas Alex, after him, and he called me Alexa Nicole as a sort of link.'

He released her and rolled over, lying with an arm across his eyes. 'Your grandmother must have had courage and determination. I don't imagine it would have been easy to bring up a child without a husband in those days.'

Stupid to feel rejected! Her skin cooling fast, Alexa said proudly, 'Not easy, but she managed.'

But she couldn't concentrate on her grandmother's sad romance. She longed to run an exploratory finger over Luka's shoulder, just for the sinful pleasure of feeling the powerful muscle contract beneath her touch, but now she felt awkward about it.

Although his tone of voice hadn't changed, she thought she'd heard the sound of doors clanging shut against her.

But those doors would never have been open for her. Even if they were, she thought with a constricted heart, she wouldn't walk through them; marrying Luka without love would be walking into hell.

Slamming the doors of her own mind on that realisation, she turned on her side and pressed her face against his arm, breathing in his scent and thrilling to the taut power that seethed through him. He dropped a kiss on the top of her head, but she could sense his absent-mindedness. That hard, forceful mind was on something else entirely.

Swallowing to ease a suspicious dry patch in her throat, she sat up. 'I'll go back to the house,' she said and clambered awkwardly out of the hammock before crouching to pick up her clothes.

Luka followed her, and from the small sounds and glimpses of his movements she deduced that he too was dressing. Chilled and clumsy, she yanked on her shirt and trousers and stuffed the rest into a pocket.

'Goodnight,' she said, hurrying away from him. He didn't try to stop her.

On the terrace outside the big living room she met the housekeeper conferring in a low voice with the security man—Danilo? No, Dion—and immediately felt that the activity of the last hour was detailed in scarlet letters on her face.

It should have been a relief when Dion barely looked at her, frowning as he asked, 'Is the Prince still down by the pool?'

'Yes, he is.' Irritated at her own prissiness, Alexa headed for the door to her bedroom. Once safely in the shower, she asked herself angrily why she should be so embarrassed.

Nowadays women made love with the men they wanted without considering themselves fallen, or even slightly tilted.

And Luka might not realise it yet, but that was the second time he'd trusted her. The first had been down at the bach, when he'd accepted her statement that she had no more cameras. Surely that meant he was beginning to—

No, she thought painfully; she couldn't let it mean anything—beyond the best sex she'd ever had.

Hoping she wasn't like her grandmother, who'd only ever loved once, she shampooed her hair, scolding herself for her choice of word.

This *couldn't* be love. She wouldn't let it be love. She

didn't know him well enough to love him. He was an arrogant, autocratic prince with an arrogant, autocratic habit of jumping to conclusions and a life that she couldn't even imagine.

But she indulged in dreamy, dazed memories until her sensuous reverie was interrupted by the discovery that she'd either left her bra behind at the pool, or dropped it on the way up to the house.

Whatever—she had to get it. She wasn't going to suffer the humiliation of having the housekeeper pick it up and present it to her. After slipping into jeans and a dark T-shirt, she made her way out of her room. Once across the terrace she sneaked into the garden and searched her way down to the darkened enclosure, feeling absurdly like a thief.

At least she didn't have to worry about the security cameras—if Luka hadn't been lying when he'd said they were turned off.

No bra gleamed on the ground, so it must still be wherever it had landed when he'd tossed it from the hammock.

Her heart settling down a little, she was just about to open the door into the pool enclosure when she heard Luka speaking in a cold, uncompromising voice that froze her breath even before he said her name.

He was speaking Dacian; frowning, she concentrated, catching words that made no sense, words that sounded like the Italian for 'I can't risk that...' and 'too much to lose...' and, shockingly, 'imprisonment.'

Flabbergasted astonishment robbed her of everything but instinct. Whatever he was talking about, it concerned her, and it wasn't good. Heart juddering, she slipped behind the lush, green bulk of some glossy-leaved shrub.

Dion answered, agreeing heartily. Cold with bewil-

derment, Alexa heard him say her name—Ms Mytton—
and ask when.

Luka hesitated a moment before answering abruptly.
Straining, Alexa translated the equivalent of, 'Let her
sleep tonight. They come tomorrow at ten, so it will have
to be before then.' He paused and added levelly, 'I'll
see to it.'

Dion started to protest, falling silent when Luka
barked one word. By then Alexa had heard enough.
Sweating and scared, her heart bumping in her throat,
she slid away from the wall and fled noiselessly back
through the darkened garden, sinister now with shadows
and menace. All the way up to the house she tried to
convince herself that she hadn't heard right, that although Dacian was very close to Italian, the words she
thought she'd heard could not possibly mean what they
seemed to.

But he'd said her name and Dion had repeated it. Even
if she'd misheard or misunderstood what they'd said,
they'd been talking about her.

Who on earth was arriving tomorrow morning?

It didn't really matter. She needed to get out of there,
and fast. She'd slip out and head for Deep Cove once
everyone was asleep. Darkness would make it much
more difficult for anyone to find her, unless they were
armed with heat-seeking equipment. And once she got
to Deep Cove she'd catch the first ferry to the mainland.
If Luka sent someone to intercept her she'd scream the
place down and demand help from the islanders.

Hardly breathing, she tiptoed into the house and slunk
into her bedroom.

Only just in time. The knock on her door arrived about
two minutes after she'd got back; she jumped, but com-

posed her face and went across. Surely he didn't expect
her to—

No. One glance at Luka's gorgeous, treacherous, *lying*
face told her that he hadn't come to make love. He
looked formal and completely self-sufficient, a dominant
man in full control of his life—a prince, not a lover, and
certainly not a man ever enslaved by his senses.

When he smiled at her and said, 'Sitting in the dark,
cara?' she felt the full impact of the barriers, the re-
moteness he hadn't shown to her after that first night in
Auckland.

She hoped she masked her pain sufficiently to fool
him. Holding her voice under such extreme discipline
that each word rasped huskily, she said, 'Just—thinking.'

His eyes narrowed slightly, but he reached out and
touched her mouth, made tender by his kisses, and for a
moment she thought she saw a shadow of regret in the
tawny eyes. 'Don't think,' he said. 'Come for a walk.'

'I'm tired,' she said with a half-smile that wobbled
before she could control it. 'Tomorrow night, perhaps?'

'It's a beautiful night, and I won't keep you for long.'

An outright refusal might make him suspicious, and
she had the whole night to make her escape. The first
ferry left at seven in the morning. Dry-mouthed, her
head buzzing, she said, 'All right, then,' and came out,
closing the door behind her.

Silently they walked out into starshine and the dark
mystery of the garden. Undercurrents, deep and turbulent
and disturbing, swirled around them in the tangy, humid
atmosphere as lights set beside the path sprang into
glowing life.

Without looking at the man beside her, Alexa gazed
about, orienting herself. Luka took her down a white
shell path they hadn't explored previously, between

high, stifling hedges to a courtyard filled with herbs and vegetables. The hedges surrounded them, rising dark enough to block out everything else but the indigo vault of the sky with its scattering of stars. In the centre of the courtyard a rose arbour still covered in blooms sheltered a fountain, softly sussurating in the humid air.

'A secret garden,' Alexa said huskily, listening to the sound of their footsteps crunching over the shell.

Alexa bent over and inhaled the scent of a rose, straightening only when her head began to spin with the dizzying perfume. A shell slid beneath her foot and she took an unexpected step sideways; Luka's hand closed around her arm as she straightened up, then dropped away.

'Careful,' he said evenly, a disturbing note of formality clipping his words. 'Come and look at the rest of the garden.'

Warily Alexa accompanied him through a narrow gate in the hedge, stepping into another charming starlit fantasy. 'How lovely,' she breathed, looking around with delight at the closely planted flowerbeds, gleaming with flowers and potent with scent.

'I thought you would like this.'

Alexa noticed a small building, embowered in shrubs. 'Is that the original homestead?' she asked, scanning the simple, practical lines of the miniature house as they walked up onto the narrow Victorian verandah, their footsteps louder and sharper on the narrow wooden boards.

Did he realise she'd overheard that frightening conversation with Dion?

No, how could he? Unless the cameras had been on— and even then he didn't know she spoke Italian well enough to understand.

'Yes. I use it as a guest-house sometimes.' He opened the door, switching on a light. 'The decorator had a wonderful time discovering original pieces for it.'

She walked in, seeing yet not seeing the tiny room, with its classical lines and furniture. Her pulses raced and adrenalin fired her with the need to get the hell out of there. Although every nerve and cell in her body was alert and on edge, she swung around and produced a fake yawn. 'It's lovely, but I'm rather tired. I'd like to go back now, Luka.'

'I'm afraid you can't.'

She froze, staring into a face carved from stone, cold and guarded as a beautiful mask.

Neatly trapped, she realised sickly. She didn't have a hope of getting to the door past him, and she had no doubt the windows were securely locked.

'I'm sorry,' he said with uncompromising determination, 'but you'll have to stay here for possibly twenty-four hours. After that you'll be free to go.'

Stunned by her own stupidity, Alexa watched him step back. But when he turned she commanded in a voice molten with fury, 'Let me out this minute or I'll scream the place down.'

'Screaming will exhaust you and achieve nothing, because the only people who'll hear you will be the men on security duty.' He paused before saying, 'I'm sorry, Alexa. At the moment I have to consider you a security risk. Please don't try to escape.'

Alexa overcame a grasping pain to demand, 'Why are you doing this? Because you still think I might leak information about you to the press?'

'Yes,' he said bluntly, and while she was still absorbing the cold, flat rejection he walked out and closed the door behind him.

Through its solid wooden depth Alexa heard the snick of a key in the lock, and a soft hiss that was almost certainly a bolt as it slid home.

So much for trust.

Still unable to believe that Luka had actually locked her in, that she was truly a prisoner, she stood motionless with bitter outrage until she was certain she was alone.

Only then, with the intense focus of a hunted animal, did she search her temporary prison. The little sitting room had one bedroom off it, with an *en suite* bathroom. Each had a window, locked and covered by wrought-iron shutters—locked also.

Alexa eyed the deadlocks with gathering frustration.

The double bed—a romantic four-poster—had been made up with linen that smelt of lavender, and on a small blanket chest at its foot stood her suitcase. She opened it, saw everything she'd brought up from Auckland neatly folded inside, along with her sponge bag. Someone had gone to the bach and collected all her clothes.

And her books. She glanced around the little room, a clever decorator's homage to a past age, and saw her computer on a side table, looking weirdly out of place.

Quickly she checked through the tiny cottage, but there was no telephone line, so she couldn't use the internet to call for help.

Face set, Alexa explored the rest of the cottage. In the tiny kitchen she dragged the door of the refrigerator open to see staples—bread, butter, cheese and milk. On the table a bowl of fruit glowed in reds and oranges and green. There were no utensils, nothing but a plastic knife, fork and spoon in the drawer. Everything was plastic, even the bowl containing the fruit and tomatoes.

Luka had anticipated exactly how she'd think. No

utensils to fashion into tools, no china to break and use, nothing metal.

A violent mixture of anguish and fear and rage churned her brain to uselessness. Luka couldn't have organised all this since she'd overheard him speak to Dion, so he'd made love to her knowing he was going to lock her in here.

Tamping her emotions down, because she had to think, to plan a way to get out of here, she continued her survey.

Each double-hung window was open at the top to let in the soft, scented air, but the deadlocks held firm, and each opening was covered by shutters. Breaking the glass wouldn't get her out.

Clearly Luka had made love to her in a cold, deliberate ploy to keep her occupied while this makeshift prison was set up.

In spite of her own complicity in the scene down by the pool, that thought hurt so much she slid hastily to another. What the *hell* was going on? Who were the mysterious 'they' he thought she might betray to the press, and what would 'they' be doing here?

She couldn't begin to think. An acute sense of bereavement, of heartshaking agony, seemed to have numbed her brain and reduced her to abject, shivering uselessness. Which was possibly exactly what Luka wanted to happen.

Galvanised into action by that humiliating suspicion, she tried the door handle again, twisting it with fruitless anger before giving up and stepping back. Even if she could pick locks there was the bolt on the outside, and for all its charming olde-worlde air the door was impregnable, held there by inset hinges and another modern deadlock.

That sly groundswell of fear chilled her skin.

So what was she going to do?

Well, she wasn't going to scream unless she knew it would get results. Luka, who'd made love to her with a fire and passion that still hummed through her body, would sedate her without a second thought.

She needed to think. Collapsing onto a delightful love seat, she fought back grief to marshal her brain into some heavy-duty scheming.

That was when she heard a helicopter coming in from the sea, low and fast, the pitch of the engine rising and steadying as it reached the house.

Who was it carrying? The 'they' who were supposed to arrive at ten tomorrow morning? Had she been imprisoned early because 'they' had changed their plans?

In spite of the best promptings of her common sense, Alexa lifted a shaking hand to her mouth as ridiculous scenarios played out in her mind.

She tried to laugh at her vivid imagination, but the emptiness beneath her breastbone and a dry mouth warned her of panic. 'Tea,' she said defiantly. 'I need a cup of tea.'

Making it gave her something to do. She was pouring it when the helicopter engine died into silence. After carrying her cup across the room, she stared out of the window and tried to think as she sipped. Luka, she decided vengefully, was going to suffer for this, if it took her all her life to come up with a suitable, satisfying revenge!

Another noise, a distant hum that rapidly turned into another helicopter, penetrated the silence. With a shaking hand she set the cup down and leaned forward, engine noise reverberating through her head. This time she saw it, lights flashing as it roared overhead and across the garden to the other side of the main house. Alexa rubbed her hand across her eyes.

Within a few minutes the harsh throbbing of the motors died into silence. Why was it so necessary for Luka to lock her away?

Bleakly she said aloud, 'I don't think it's because the Prince is coy about having a woman in his house. If I'm a security risk, these people must be here on highly secret business.'

Who were they? Slowly she finished the tea while she worried away at the puzzle.

Could it be a meeting of tycoons and captains of industry?

It didn't seem likely. By locking her up, Luka had to know he'd set himself up for charges of abduction and imprisonment, so whoever had arrived in those helicopters had to be hugely important—and possibly here on a matter of life and death.

Somehow business tycoons gathering to plot bigger and better takeovers didn't fit.

Diplomats? But why would the ruler of an Adriatic island nation be negotiating weighty international affairs in New Zealand?

Which left her with a much more sinister suspicion.

Was he involved in something illegal?

No. Not Luka. Irrational though it was in the light of his recent behaviour, she knew without even thinking about it that he wouldn't step across that line.

So what on earth was so hush-hush it had forced him to stoop to kidnapping? The only thing she could think of was the welfare of his people. If that was at risk, then, yes, she could see Luka doing whatever had to be done.

Gazing around the neat, ordinary room, she couldn't hold back a half-sob. Here she was, talking herself into the dangerous syndrome of finding excuses for Luka's behaviour because the alternative explanation—that he'd coolly, cynically betrayed her—hurt too much.

'Well, if you thought you might be falling in love with him,' she muttered, wincing at the brittle note in her voice, 'you've learned a lesson.'

Her gaze fell on a pile of magazines neatly stacked on a polished wooden table.

A suspicious warmth flooded through her, which she banished by saying aloud, 'The amenable Ms Martin probably thought of it. Amazing what some people will do to earn their living!'

She wouldn't be able to concentrate on a magazine, or any of the books from a tall bookshelf against one wall, so she washed the cup and saucer, surprised when a yawn caught her unexpectedly. A grey flood of exhaustion poured through her, weighting her bones and dulling her mind, but she set her jaw and went over the house with painstaking care, searching for some weakness she could exploit. She was not going to meekly remain a prisoner without at least trying to escape.

Much later, she had to admit defeat. She'd failed to pick the locks with her nail file, and there was nothing in the place she could use as a means of prying open the shutters or smashing the locks.

Smothering her torment with anger, she discarded any thought of changing into nightclothes and stretched out on the bed, staring into the darkness while futile, anguished suppositions raced through her mind. She listened for sounds that never came, until eventually she slept.

Alexa opened heavy eyelids to light, and bewilderment. For long moments her sluggish mind tried to work out where on earth she was. She swallowed several times to ease a throat like sandpaper, before finally deciding she needed a drink.

It was strangely difficult to force herself up from the bed, and when she stood at last she had to grab the back of the chair to stop herself from falling. Her head spun and her legs didn't want to know her.

She had, she realised, been crying in her sleep.

And of course it hadn't been a dream—Luka really had made love to her and betrayed her...

Biting her lip, she stumbled into the bathroom and washed her face. A glance at her watch revealed that it was six-thirty in the morning. She poured a glass of water and drank it down greedily, relishing its coolness, then went back into the bedroom and crawled under the sheets again.

Lying with one hand behind her head, she stared across at the window. The more she thought about her situation, the more she began to believe that Luka had intentionally used sex to control her.

Bitter chagrin roiled through her in an icy, humiliating wave. She'd been so blind, so easily tricked.

Alexa knew she'd inherited her father's good bones and her mother's superb skin, knew that her large eyes, pale as crystals beneath their sleepy, cat-like lids, fascinated some men. Yet even those assets, and the long legs and small, high breasts that helped her look good in her clothes, couldn't compare with the beautiful, sophisticated women Luka had been linked to.

She'd known that, but she'd wilfully throttled every forewarning, every instinct that had warned her to be careful. Overwhelmed by her first taste of heroic passion, she'd surrendered without a bleat, eagerly letting herself be duped by Luka's charisma and the dark sexuality that pulsed beneath his sophisticated charm.

She couldn't have made it easier for him if she'd tried.

Disgusted with herself, she muttered, 'Face it, you dumped your common sense and self-control. For a man who makes love like a god.'

A gentle curve of colour on the bedside table caught her eye. Frowning, she levered herself up on one elbow and saw a flower. Cool and soft as tissue paper, it had been tucked between two scented green feijoas—fruit she loved and had eaten with pleasure at the breakfast she'd shared with Luka.

Holding her breath, she reached out and picked up the flower, shivering when she felt the dampness of the dew still on its soft white petals.

A cotton rose.

Her throat closed up. Was it a mute apology?

No, she thought, struggling against a weak need to be reassured. Luka had made love to her in a deliberate attempt to throw her off balance. This would be the same—a lying promise of something he had no intention of delivering.

Or a taunt.

How dared he come into her room, watch her sleeping, and drop flowers and fruit beside her?

Mortified, she wondered whether he'd witnessed the tears that had been choking her when she finally woke.

She stormed out into the kitchen, pushing back the curtains as she went to let sunlight into the rooms. The lush cottage garden rioted in a profuse display of colour and form between the hedges that blocked out everything else, even the sea.

She pulled down a packet of cereal and stood with it

in her hand while her eyes stung with foolish tears. The cereal was her favourite.

'So?' she demanded, and poured some into a bowl. She didn't feel hungry but she'd eat, because she needed to keep her strength up.

When the plastic plate was empty, she forced herself to drink coffee, and after that to work on the genealogy program on her computer, filling in a day that dragged slowly by, silent and peaceful except for an occasional bark from the caretaker's dog and the ever-present feeling of being under surveillance.

Some time during the following night she was woken by the *thud-thud-thud* of the helicopters. Definitely two, she realised as she lay rigid on the bed, listening with every sense on full alert.

CHAPTER NINE

AFTER a paralysed moment Alexa scrambled off the bed. What was going to happen now?

She'd already worked out what she was going to do; moving as silently as she could, she raced out to stand behind the door so that Luka couldn't see her when he opened it. Yesterday after he'd left she'd carried a chair there. It had seemed light enough then, and how many times had she seen people on the screen lift a chair without even breathing heavily?

Probably thousands, but now the chair was heavy and uncooperative, and although she'd practised doing it several times she felt an utter fool with it hoisted above her head.

Pulses skipping and shallow, she listened as the choppers lifted and flew out to sea. A huge relief took her by surprise.

She didn't hear him come, didn't hear the bolt being drawn or the lock click, but a subtle alteration in the atmosphere warned her strained senses that he was there.

The door eased back, stopping just short of where she stood. To her intense chagrin he stayed on the doorstep.

Could he hear her breathing? No, because she wasn't. So what had warned him—the sound of her heart bounding unevenly in her throat?

She nearly screamed when Luka laughed. 'I should have guessed,' he said drily, and switched on the light. 'A chair?' he said, amusement still showing in his tone and his eyes.

140

'It seemed a good idea at the time,' Alexa snarled, white with rage.

She put down the chair and stepped out from behind the door. Head held high, she stared at him, her anger and aggression transmuting into concern the moment she realised that his olive skin stretched tautly over the strong framework of his face and there were dark shadows beneath his golden eyes. He looked as though he hadn't slept at all since she'd seen him last.

'It was a good idea, but you don't need to protect yourself.' All amusement scoured from his voice, he said flatly, 'It's over, Alexa. You're free. And one day I hope you'll forgive me for locking you up like this.'

He was leaving the country—leaving her. She could tell it although his tone revealed nothing. *I do not care,* she thought defiantly, while her heart twisted in denial.

'What time is it?' she demanded.

'An hour before dawn. Do you want to go back to the bach, or to Auckland?'

'To Auckland,' she said quickly, adding, 'But first I want to know what the hell is going on.'

He paused. 'I can't tell you.'

'You mean you don't trust me.' She gave a cynical little laugh. 'But what's new about that?' Good enough to make love to, just not good enough to trust.

His silence confirmed it. She drew in a sharp breath, but before she could speak he said abruptly, 'I would like to trust you, but I cannot. It is not—' He stopped, then finished with icy composure, 'It is not just you. I learned early in my life that a prince can trust no one— not his mother, not his father, not his best friend. I ask you to believe that I would never have behaved like an arrogant despot if people's lives had not been at risk.'

Lives? She must have said it aloud, because he said,

'Yes. And although it will infuriate you, I must ask you to trust me.'

She threw him a seething glare. 'Why should I?'

Luka shrugged as he admitted, 'There is no reason why you should, but this—problem is not over yet. Will you remain quiet about it, at least for a week?'

She flashed, 'So that the police will ask me why I didn't complain immediately?'

'Think that if you like,' he said indifferently, watching her from narrowed eyes. 'A week, Alexa. That's all I ask. You say I don't trust you, but there is no trust in you, either.'

She hesitated. 'And if I say no?'

'Then you'll have to stay here,' he said calmly. 'Not locked up, but as my guest in the house.'

'But if I say I won't tell anyone you'll trust me enough to let me go?'

He paused. She could sense the reluctance radiating from him when he eventually said, 'Yes.'

And even though Alexa knew she was being reck-lessly stupid, she muttered, 'All right.'

'Thank you.'

Setting her teeth, she said flatly, 'Well, goodbye.'

He didn't move. 'Goodbye, Alexa. Is there anything I can do—?'

'No!'

His hand closed over hers; he pulled her into him and kissed her. It started off in sweet and seducing tender-ness, to be transformed into a passion so violent her knees buckled. Aware only that this was goodbye, Alexa pressed herself against him until, sick with shame, she jerked away.

'I'm sorry,' he said, letting her go. His voice was level and aloof; clearly he hadn't felt anything like the bitter yearning that clawed her. 'For everything. I hope you have a very happy life, Alexa. Try not to think of me with hatred.'

He turned, and some minutes later, still standing rigidly in the dark, she heard the sound of another helicopter start up.

So he'd put off releasing her until the very last moment. Tears ached behind her eyes, clogged her throat, but if she started to cry now she might never stop. After pushing the door wide open, she went to get her suitcase.

Scrabbling for her key, Alexa said patiently, 'No, Sean, I don't want to make you a cup of coffee.'

Her companion for the evening laughed and grabbed her wrist, using his superior strength to turn her around. 'Come on, Alexa, don't be so stuffy.'

Irritated into discarding her usual tact, she snapped, 'I don't want to kiss you either. And I certainly don't want to go to bed with you.' With a sharp twist she wrenched free. 'Goodnight. Don't keep the taxi waiting.'

Her escort had drunk just enough to make him stubborn. 'Why?' he persisted. 'I like you and you like me— what's your problem?'

Another figure loomed behind him at the top of the steps. Although Alexa's eyes dilated, she immediately discounted her response; a couple of achingly lonely months hadn't been long enough for her to overcome the tendency to see Luka in every tall, dark man.

But when the newcomer said in familiar, deadly tones, '*You* are the problem,' Alexa's heart skidded to a stop.

Frozen, she saw Sean swing around, jaw jutting as he confronted Luka. 'Who the hell are you?' he demanded.

'Nobody you'd be interested in,' Luka returned curtly. He looked past Sean to Alexa. 'Do you want him gone?'

Straining to keep a wild, incredulous hope from her voice, she unglued her tongue enough to croak, 'He's going.'

But Sean said belligerently, 'Like hell I am. I was here first.'

In the voice that probably sent shivers down the spines of his underlings, Luka responded, 'You heard her.'

The naked, brutal authority in his tone and stance got through to Sean. Shrugging, he walked past and stamped down the steps. A safe distance away, he flung over his shoulder, 'You should have told me there was a man in your life, Alexa. I don't poach.'

Unfortunately he spoilt the bravado of his exit by tripping. Tense and unbearably expectant, Alexa kept her eyes on him as he moved faster than strictly necessary to the waiting cab.

Silence stretched between the two outside the door until she broke it by saying, 'Thank you,' in a flat, strained voice.

'Who is he?' Luka asked indifferently.

'A friend,' she returned, cutting it short because the words stumbled off her tongue. Embarrassment warring with an exultant hope, she kept her eyes on the key as she thrust it into the lock and turned it.

'Do all your friends make passes at you?'

If it hadn't been for the cold distaste in his tone she might have suspected jealousy, but this was no returning lover come to sweep her off her feet into a sensual idyll.

'That,' she told him, her heart plummeting, 'is none of your business. But as it happens, no, they don't. And Sean won't try it again.'

A car door slammed and both turned to watch the taxi drive away with its resentful burden.

'I need to see you,' Luka said, looming tall and dark and ominous against the diffused lights from the street.

'Now?' Another squeaky word—he'd think she was mad. She coughed and resumed, 'It's after midnight.'

'It's important.'

Shivering, she pushed the door open and muttered, 'You'd better come in.'

What state was the flat in? She couldn't remember, and as they walked without speaking along the hall she hoped it was tidy.

Not too bad, she realised, casting a swift glance around as Luka closed the door behind him. At least there were flowers—a huge bunch of southern tulips holding up brilliant scarlet chalices. She'd bought them that afternoon because everything else in her life seemed grey.

And now the cause of her nagging, ever-present misery was in her home, watching her with icy detachment.

Skin prickling, she asked stiffly, 'How long have you been in Auckland?'

'I flew in this evening,' he told her, all cool authority, watching her with hooded eyes and a poker face. 'On a private visit.'

She sent him a glittering glance. 'I won't tell anyone,' she said curtly, because she wanted more than anything to ask if he'd come alone, or with the latest royal princess to take his fancy. According to the gossipmongers, this one was serious; Luka had stayed with her family in their château in France.

His eyes narrowed. 'I know.'

Overcoming a foolish desire to hold her breath, she asked, 'Did I finally manage to convince you that I wasn't a member of the paparazzi?'

His smile was assured and lethal. 'Yes.'

Deliberately she opened her eyes wide. 'How?'

'You didn't sell photographs or a story. And you kept your promise not to talk.'

It would have been wiser to remain silent, yet she couldn't prevent herself from saying, 'I don't renege on promises.' And because that sounded self-righteous, she hurried on, 'Thank you for replacing my father's camera. It must have taken some searching to find an identical one.'

He shrugged. 'It was nothing.'

Which probably meant he'd told some minion to find it and post it off to her, although he had signed the note that came with it. 'It meant a lot to me.'

'And you have already thanked me in a formal little note,' he said.

Which he hadn't answered. Because that still stung, she asked quietly, 'Did you organise the chance for me to work with Trudi Jerkin?'

That had come out of the blue: a week spent escorting one of the world's best photographers around New Zealand. She had learnt so much.

Watching Luka closely, Alexa saw the betraying quiver of his lashes and said briskly, 'I'm very grateful, but you don't owe me anything, you know. The day I read about the peace treaty in Sant'Rosa I understood why you'd been so antagonistic at having me wave cameras around right next door.'

When the news had broken, with the information that the treaty had been hammered out at Luka's beach house, Alexa had devoured everything she could find about it. One article she'd even cut out and hidden in her drawer.

Prince Luka, the journalist had written, was a man whose combination of old-world diplomatic skill, ruthless intelligence, charm and a brilliant financial mind were far more important than his rank—although in status-conscious Pacific societies that was no disadvantage.

By arranging this treaty the Bank of Dacia had gained considerable influence in the Pacific-Asian region. It had also set in motion the re-opening of the huge and lucrative mines closed by the fighting—and that too would be good for the Bank.

And for Dacia.

'I was on my way to meet representatives from the Sant'Rosan government when you were almost attacked,' Luka said, his tone as aloof as his expression. 'The government insisted on secrecy because the neighbouring state was ready to invade.'

Alexa nodded. Of course he would sympathise with a small state threatened by foreign troops.

He gave her a keen glance. 'The Sant'Rosans wanted a peace-keeping force in position before news of any treaty leaked out.'

Alexa loosened fingers laced so tightly together that they were almost white. 'I do understand why you felt the need for secrecy on the island—I even understand why you thought I might have links to that wretched gossip columnist—who turned out, incidentally, to have a mole in Carole's office who listened to phone calls—but I still think that locking me up was a huge overreaction.'

Luka said crisply, 'It seemed appropriate action at the time. I know that a prison is a prison, however comfortable it is, but I would do it again if I had to. I hoped that you would realise how little I enjoyed being forced to do it.'

Skin burned along her cheekbones as she remembered

the cotton rose. 'It doesn't matter,' she said in a cool voice. 'The peace treaty seems to be holding, so it was worthwhile.'

He hesitated, then said quietly, 'Sit down, Alexa. I have something to tell you.'

Alexa surveyed him with a mutinous glint, but obeyed, deliberately folding her hands in her lap. Just like that, the subject was finished with!

She glanced at his serious, stern face through her lashes, and with a sudden appalled leap of foreboding wondered if he'd come all this way to inform her that he was going to marry his exiled princess.

Why would he bother? They'd shared nothing but sex and sparring. 'Fire away,' she said tightly.

In a dispassionate, almost neutral voice he said, 'When we first met, your eyes fascinated me.'

Whatever she'd expected to hear, it wasn't this. Incredulously she repeated, 'My *eyes*?'

His mouth tightened. 'Amongst other things,' he drawled, leaving her in no doubt what those other things were. Ignoring the hot colour staining her skin, he went on, 'I have a friend with eyes exactly the same colour. I had other things to think of, so I put the coincidence from my mind. However, when you told me your father was half-Italian, and that you didn't know who your grandfather was, I became intrigued.'

'Why?' The word sounded clumsy and she realised she was holding her breath.

'My friend comes from that part of the world.'

The colour drained from Alexa's skin. Unable to speak, she stared at him, greedily noting the way the warm lamplight coaxed shades of amber and gold from the skin stretched taut over his slashing cheekbones.

Impassively Luka continued, 'Even though you bear

his names in Anglicised form, that is not so unusual—
Alexa and Nicole have been fashionable for some time
now. But when you told me they were your father's
names, and that his father had been your grandmother's
lover at an Italian university, I was intrigued. Back in
Dacia I set a researcher to find out what he could about
your grandmother's sojourn in Italy.'

'You had no right to do that,' she said stonily. 'You
don't have to pay me back somehow for locking me up.
You should have told me what you suspected, and I
could have decided what to do.'

His brows snapped together. 'There are other considerations,' he told her.

'What considerations?'

'The identity of the man who was your grandfather.'

Alexa's breath blocked her throat. Swallowing, she
said huskily, 'You found him?'

He slipped a lean, elegant hand into his pocket and
pulled out a photograph, laying it down on the coffee
table in front of her. 'Do you recognise these people?'

She gazed at it, hands clenching in her lap. 'Yes,' she
said huskily, staring at the couple who smiled at each
other in the faded snapshot. 'I've got one very like it.'

'May I see it?'

Dizzy with a mixture of anticipation and anguish, she
raced into her bedroom and brought out two framed photographs from her dressing table. 'My grandparents,' she
said, showing him the older one, 'and my parents. You
can see a family resemblance between my—my grandfather and my father.'

Luka's hard, handsome face didn't change expression
as he scrutinised them. He put them down and said,
'Yes. It all fits together very well.'

'So who was he? My grandfather?'

Incredibly, Luka said, 'It seems that at the time he met your grandmother he was the Crown Prince of Illyria. DNA testing would prove it, but all the information points to that.'

Alexa's jaw dropped. When she could speak again she said faintly, 'The one who married a New Zealand woman? No, he's too young!'

'Not Prince Alex but his father, then Crown Prince Nicolo.' Luka watched her intently. 'He met your grandmother at university in Italy and they became lovers. When her year of study was over she returned to New Zealand, pregnant with your father. Prince Nicolo can't have known because by all accounts he had an over-developed sense of responsibility, and I think he'd have supported her and his child at the very least.'

'It sounds like a fairy story,' Alexa said thinly, trying to sort her whirling thoughts. She bunched her hands into fists to stop them shaking. 'Too far-fetched.'

'There had to be a reason for your grandmother, who sounds a sensible and loving woman, to keep all knowledge of her son's father from him.' Luka touched Alexa's photograph. 'That man with your grandmother is definitely the present Prince of Illyria's father at the age of twenty. If your grandmother understood that in the climate of the times there was no chance of them marrying, her decision makes sense.'

'And she wouldn't have wanted to burden him with the knowledge of an illegitimate child,' Alexa said numbly. 'What happened to him when Illyria was overrun?'

'After that year in Italy he went on to university in Switzerland and Great Britain. He married just before the communist upheaval and worked secretly as a peasant in his country until he, his wife and his son Alex, now Prince of Illyria and your half-uncle, were betrayed. He died giving his wife and son time to escape.'

Alexa blinked back sudden, painful tears for a man she had never known.

'Yes, he was a hero,' Luka said quietly. 'You have every right to be proud of him.'

Alexa swallowed. 'I—don't know what to say.'

He laughed quietly. 'For perhaps the first time in our acquaintanceship.'

She bit her lip fiercely to stop it trembling. 'Why did you go to all this trouble?'

'It seemed the least I could do to make up for the indignities I subjected you to. You said that you had a hole in your life. And although you laughed when you talked of a big Italian family, you sounded wistful.'

He sounded almost bored. Another man with a strongly developed sense of responsibility, she decided painfully, because it would have meant so much if he'd done this to please her, instead of making amends.

'I—thank you,' she said, hiding the uncertainty in her words with an attempt at briskness.

'You don't need to thank me,' he returned negligently. His face hardening into a cold, bronze mask, he went on, 'Unfortunately, while researching this, my employee was careless enough to alert someone else to the possibility of a child sired by Nicolo. That information was handed on.'

Feeling extremely sorry for the careless employee, Alexa asked, 'To whom?'

'The royal family of Illyria.'

Alexa's head came up. Her eyes met his, fire duelling with ice. Lashes falling, she looked away. 'I see.' She waited, and when he said nothing she murmured, 'I don't imagine it matters. It doesn't seem likely that they'll be terribly interested in an unknown relative on the other side of the world.' It was one thing to fantasise occasionally about a large, happy Italian family; it was quite another to be presented with the reality of a royal half-uncle.

'You do Alex a disservice,' Luka said austerely. 'He is extremely interested. He contacted me, and when he realised that I had met you he asked if I could arrange a meeting.'

'A meeting?' Alexa echoed, limp with shock. So this was why he'd come.

She swallowed a lump in her throat to croak, 'Why?'

'He wants to meet you,' Luka said coolly. 'He suggested Dacia as a neutral place for that meeting. His wife is pregnant, and travelling is uncomfortable for her, but she can cope with a flight from Illyria to Dacia.'

'Dacia?' Hope, ever-present, undying, burst into life again. To quell it, she asked, 'Why Dacia?'

'It would cause too much interest in Illyria if an unknown woman with the Considine eyes and bone structure arrived there,' he told her curtly. 'Press photographers and gutter journalists would gather from around the world, sniffing out a story.'

'Is there no freedom of the press in Dacia?' she asked with a spark of malice.

He gave a narrow, cynical smile. 'My people are more accustomed to me than the Illyrians are to Alex—they allow me a private life. Outsiders I can ban, if necessary.'

Mind churning, Alexa unfroze enough to pace across to the window. Pulling back the curtain to stare into the small courtyard garden outside, she said indistinctly, 'I hadn't—it's so clichéd to think there might be royalty in your ancestry, and I certainly didn't expect to find it in mine! I don't know that I want to meet this so-called uncle of mine.'

'That's a decision only you can make,' Luka said coolly.

Chilled by his remote courtesy, she was goaded into indiscretion. Turning her head, she ignored the constriction of her heart to raise mocking brows. 'No more kidnapping, Luka?'

Tension suddenly sparked into the air. Don't be a fool, Alexa told herself. She should have learned by now that pricking at his self-control was futile.

Without moving he said abruptly, 'I hated locking you up, but I couldn't run the risk of letting you go free. Too much was at stake. I have a young cousin who is an adventurer—still reckless and eager. Somehow he managed to wangle a trip to Sant'Rosa on a ship full of medical supplies. He was recognised, and kept there as a hostage.'

'Why?' Dropping the curtain, she turned back into the room, her hands suddenly shaky. 'I seem to be saying that every second word. What happened—is he all right?'

He shrugged. 'Yes. When I told you that lives depended on your silence, his was one. The Sant'Rosans were desperate men, and they used him to force me to work for them and do it in secrecy.' He gave a hard smile. 'When I arrived to talk to the guerrilla forces—'

Horrified, she breathed, 'You went to Sant'Rosa after you left the beach? You walked into the middle of a civil war?'

'It was necessary,' he said, watching her with cool amber eyes.

'You could have been killed!'

'They needed reassurance.' As though the words were

torn from him he said, 'I understand men who don't trust anyone, not even their leaders.'

'I know.' She was holding her breath.

'My parents' marriage was—difficult. I grew up knowing that my mother was not a Dacian, that her interests lay elsewhere. It taught me not to rely on anyone but myself.'

That feeling of balancing on the edge of a precipice increased. 'I'm so sorry,' she said, thinking of a small boy with no one to turn to.

'Neither of them wished for the marriage. My mother had been forced onto my father, and he onto her, and she was both spy and hostage. Yet they loved me.'

And he had been the child in the middle, unable to bridge the gap. Tentatively Alexa said, 'It must have been hell for both of them.'

'It got worse when my father decided that I should be initiated into my duties as ruler. He warned me clearly that I could not speak to my mother about anything that I learned.' His voice was cold, as cold as the frozen fire veiled by his lashes. 'And then of course the media circus began when I reached eighteen. I grew to despise and distrust all journalists and photographers. Alexa, I dared not tell you what was going on—premature disclosure of the peace talks could have derailed the whole process and led to the death of my cousin.'

For the first time he was revealing something of himself to her. Alexa treasured every difficult word, even as she ached with sympathy.

She managed to smile and said cheerfully, 'At first I had every intention of getting even with you when I finally got out of that cell. But when I read about the treaty—well, a few hours spent locked up didn't mean much compared to the misery the Sant'Rosans have endured for so long. It was a comfortable cell.'

'My mother spent her life in a very comfortable cell,' he said with sombre intensity. 'In the end her lack of freedom killed her.'

Alexa said again, 'I'm so sorry.'

Hard eyes searched her face. 'Yes, I think you are,' he said with a twisted smile. 'It all happened a long time ago. When you come to Dacia I'll make a villa available where you and your half-uncle will have privacy. You need not see me at all.'

He couldn't have made his lack of interest in her more obvious.

Pierced to the quick, she said woodenly, 'I can't just up and go—I have a job.'

'Can't you spare a week? I will make all the arrangements—it won't cost you anything,' he said, a muscle tightening in his jaw. 'Perhaps this letter from Alex will persuade you.' He produced an envelope from his pocket and handed it to her.

Accepting it from him, Alexa bit her lip. Luka certainly wasn't trying to persuade her! His barriers were slammed firmly into place.

'Read it,' he commanded, a hint of impatience roughening the deep voice.

Alexa opened the envelope and unfolded the single sheet of paper to see what the Prince of Illyna had written.

Dear Alexa Mytton,
My wife and I would very much like to meet you, and as I know this is at very short notice I've asked my good friend Luka to deliver this. If you can come to see us, give him the dates so I can organise your

tickets. For obvious reasons I must ask you not to let anyone else but those you trust know about this.

He was hers, Alex Considine.

Alexa looked up into remote eyes. 'Why you? It's a long way from Dacia to New Zealand.'

'Not so long from Asia, where I've been for the past week. As for coming—it was my fault that your private story was made public in however minor a degree. And after discussing it we decided that you would prefer to hear this news from someone you know.'

Had he told the Prince of Illyria that he'd made love to her? Alexa cast a fleeting glance at his beautiful, disciplined face and shivered inwardly, repressing the erotic images that flashed across her mind. Why should he? It had meant nothing more than momentary physical pleasure.

And the sooner she realised that and gave up her pathetic dreams, the better it would be for her.

Before she could think of a reply he said, 'I'll leave you now to make up your mind. I'm flying to Sant'Rosa in an hour, but I'll ring you at eight tomorrow morning.' He smiled at her, amused, ironic, without humour. 'Even if you decide not to go to Dacia this will not be the end; Alex is a very determined man, and he wants to meet you.'

After she'd closed the door behind him Alexa felt light-headed, almost drunk with pleasure at seeing Luka again—yet the ice that had been building inside her since she'd left the island had advanced some more. He'd made it so plain he didn't want any contact between them.

He had looked tired, she thought anxiously, his strong features more angular and the dark energy that drummed through him a little less forceful than before. Had he been working too hard?

Stupid to care...

Alexa spent the rest of that night lying awake in the dark, listening to traffic noises. She didn't have to make up her mind—she knew what her answer was going to be. She'd spent two months trying to get Luka out of her mind, and will-power hadn't worked. Now was her chance to see if harsh reality might do the trick. According to the headlines, his exiled princess had been shopping in Paris for a trousseau.

Perhaps the tiredness she'd read in his face was simply sexual exhaustion.

To her he'd never been a prince, with all that that status implied—he'd simply been a man. Surely seeing him in his natural habitat would force her wilful heart to recognise the stupidity of hope.

And perhaps meeting her new family might ease this constant nagging grief, this longing for something she could never have, for a man who'd never love her.

CHAPTER TEN

A MONTH later Alexa was sitting inside a jet on the runway at the only international airfield on Dacia. When she'd gone to pay for her flight she'd discovered that it was already paid for, and when she'd embarked she'd realised that either Luka or her unknown uncle had booked her first class all the way.

She'd repay whoever it was, even if it broke her.

Buoyed by a stomach-churning mixture of tiredness and pulsing, heady excitement, she peered through the window. From the air Dacia had spread a green and white patchwork in a brilliant sea. Groves of trees lay like silvery fur over the central spine of hills, and beaches looped in silver crescents between high white headlands. Some of those headlands, she'd noted with a surge of excitement, were crowned with what looked to be castles.

Swallowing hard, Alexa picked up her hand luggage and followed the rest of the travellers out into the terminal.

'Ms Mytton?' a voice enquired.

Alexa looked at the smiling young woman who accosted her, and nodded. 'I'm Alexa Mytton,' she confirmed.

'I am Lucia Bagaton, and I have been sent to meet you. Please come this way.'

Alexa followed her through a door to a small, private lounge where she was reunited with her luggage before being whisked out of another door and into a car so rapidly she gained only an impression of hot sunlight, and the scent of the sea mingling with the pungent odour of aircraft fuel.

Immediately the door had closed behind them the car sped away, its tinted windows hiding the passengers from any curious gaze.

Alexa sank back as they drove away from the airport, listening to her escort's running commentary on the vineyards and olive groves. Clearly Lucia Bagaton, who had to be some relative of Luka's, didn't expect an answer.

But when Alexa gave a sharp exclamation, and twisted in her seat to stare at a honey-coloured building across a vine-patterned field, her companion said, 'That is a pre-Romanesque church built over a thousand years ago. Lovely, isn't it?'

'I've never seen such an old building,' Alexa said, gazing at it until olive trees cut off her sight. The car avoided a woman on a donkey, who waved and called out a smiling greeting.

'You are interested in antiquities?' At Alexa's nod, Lucia Bagaton said, 'We have Greek and Roman ruins here also. Perhaps you will get to see some.'

Carefully Alexa said, 'Forgive me, but are you related to L—the Prince of Dacia?'

Lucia Bagaton gave her an equally careful smile. 'A distant cousin,' she said. 'I work for him as an occasional social secretary.'

The car turned onto a much narrower road that threaded between stone walls and a pine forest until it stopped in front of elaborately wrought iron gates. The driver sounded the horn, and as Alexa watched the gates swung back, opening the way between high walls faded to a dusty, delightful apricot.

'This is the villa Luka thought you might like to stay in,' her escort said as the car eased through. She flashed a cool, professional smile at Alexa. 'You will be completely private here.'

After supervising the man who carried Alexa's bags up to a cool bedroom, shuttered against the fierce sun and the glare from the sea, she turned to Alexa and said, 'Enjoy your stay, Ms Mytton. I'd suggest a short rest, then perhaps a swim. Dinner will be served in two hours. If you need anything, ask Carlotta, the housekeeper, who will contact me. And if you wish to do any sightseeing I will be more than happy to arrange it for you and accompany you. Goodbye.'

Not exactly dismissive—very gracious, in fact—but there was a barrier there. It could be a family characteristic, or might his distant cousin perhaps be in love with Luka?

'Thank you,' Alexa said with a smile that faded into bleakness as the door closed behind her escort.

Luka had made it obvious that he didn't want to resume any sort of relationship, so it was stupid to feel abandoned. She straightened her shoulders and looked around, remembering another bedroom beside another sea. Both tiled and sparsely furnished, they couldn't have been more different. Equally beautiful and suited to the climate, this room bore the imprint of an ancient culture in the thick walls and heavy carved furniture.

Fighting a ridiculous forlornness, Alexa showered in the small marble bathroom off the bedroom, staying under the cool spray until her skin began to wrinkle. When she came back to the bedroom she found her case unpacked and her clothes hidden in a huge armoire that smelt of lavender and rosemary.

The homely scents reassured her. Surrendering to

tiredness, she lay down on the daybed and wooed her brain into quietude as the sunlight smouldering through the shutters dwindled into a copper glow.

Her brain obstinately refused to drift, embarking again on a familiar treadmill of queries and yearning hopes.

'Oh, grow up!' she exclaimed furiously, moving restlessly on the pile of pillows.

Luka was making it more than clear that whatever they'd shared was dead for him. So it had better die for her too. Obsessing about him was a waste of time and emotional energy.

Impatient with her foolishness, she finally got up and chose a long, floaty skirt in the finest cotton, pairing it with a sleeveless shell top in the same pale blue. She combed her hair back from her face and applied lipstick before walking down the stairs, feeling like a trespasser in the big, silent house.

Without looking at any of the rooms, she found her way onto a terrace at the back of the house, shaded by pink bougainvillaea. A pang of homesickness brought tears aching to her eyes.

Forcing herself to appear calm, she walked across to a keyhole window in the wall through which she glimpsed an alluring cascade of more bougainvillaea— scarlet this time. Enchanted, every sense vibrant and alert, she peered into a courtyard with palms in pots and a lily-dotted pool. Someone had set a table there—for two, she noticed, and suddenly her heart thundered in her breast and she felt alive again.

'Good evening.'

Alexa swung around. Luka stood at the door of the house, tall and dark, in trousers tailored to fit his lean hips and long legs and a white shirt with sleeves rolled up.

Absurdly glad she'd decided to wear her prettiest casual clothes, she said unevenly, 'Hello.' Oh, you've got it bad, she thought disgustedly, but her tremulous smile refused to go away.

Golden gaze fixed to her face, he came out onto the terrace. 'I hope everything is to your satisfaction,' he said formally.

Now it was. With enormous reluctance Alexa admitted that whatever she felt for him was more than desire, more than fascination—much, much more.

Resisting the implications, she said, 'I'd be very hard to please if it wasn't. This is lovely, thank you.' After a moment's hesitation she asked, 'When will—the Prince of Illyria come?'

'The day after tomorrow,' Luka told her, his deep voice laconic. 'We thought it best to give you a complete day to recover from the flight.' His eyes narrowing, he scrutinised her face. 'That doesn't please you?'

Alexa said, 'No, no, it's fine. This is the first time I've flown for more than six hours, but I don't think I'm jet-lagged. Do long flights affect you?'

'No,' he said calmly. 'I've trained myself to sleep and I drink vast amounts of water.'

'Which reminds me,' she said, 'I owe you for the flight.'

He grinned. 'Shall we quarrel about that tomorrow? This is your first night here, and I'd like you to enjoy it.'

Taken aback, Alexa said, 'I hadn't planned to quarrel!'

'So forget about it.' At her hesitation, he said lazily, 'Until tomorrow.'

'Until tomorrow,' she agreed recklessly, aware that

when he looked at her like that she'd forget anything he asked her to.

'Sit down and tell me how the flight went,' he said, going across to the table that held, she was surprised to see, a bottle of champagne and two flutes, glittering in the candlelight.

What was he up to? she wondered, trying very hard to be cynical, and failing. Excitement hollowed out her stomach, zinging along her nerve-ends like an electric current that played by its own rules.

As the sky filled with strange stars and the wind whispered across the pines, Luka poured out champagne and handed her a flute before suggesting a toast to reunions.

'Reunions,' Alexa said ironically, and sipped the golden liquid. 'Although it's not exactly a reunion—I haven't met Prince Alex before.'

'He looks enough like your father to make it one,' Luka said, his smile wry.

'He certainly does. Now that I know, I'm astonished I didn't notice before,' she said lightly.

'Because you weren't expecting to see it.'

'That must be it.' Casting about for something else to say, Alexa asked about Sant'Rosa.

Luka began to talk of the situation there. Telling herself firmly that she was glad he avoided any personal topics, she listened, her tension easing a little. She could, she thought despairingly, spend the night discussing the affairs of the world with him.

Dinner arrived, delivered on a trolley by the beaming housekeeper, who then disappeared. Over a superb meal they continued to talk, a stimulated Alexa hungrily drinking in the sound of Luka's deep voice, the way he smiled, the mellow gleam of candlelight on his strong features, his lithe male grace.

Afterwards, in the big bed in her room, Alexa replayed the conversation over in her mind, awed by his responsibilities, impressed by his acute grasp of world affairs, and fascinated by his absolute discretion, because he'd told her nothing she hadn't already read or heard in the media.

In spite of his statement in Auckland, he still didn't trust her. It didn't seem likely that he'd ever overcome that childhood conditioning.

Hopeless and unhappy, she thumped her pillow and buried her hot face in it.

But he still wanted her. Able to control almost everything else, he couldn't hide the small physical signs of awareness and desire—the flick of a muscle in his jaw and the dilating pupils that turned his eyes to smouldering topaz gems when he looked at her.

She pressed her hand against her racing heart and told it sternly to stop.

However susceptible to Luka's raw male charm, she couldn't be in love with him. Although memories of their lovemaking still had the power to send ripples of thwarted passion through her, and any relationship with him would be explosive and wild and heart-stoppingly passionate, he'd never lose control—and she'd always know that for her it was second-best.

And she certainly wasn't suitable mistress material.

'Anyway, it's academic,' she told the silent room. He hadn't made one move towards her during the evening— had carefully avoided touching her, had skilfully and ruthlessly kept the conversation on impersonal matters.

He'd probably hoot with laughter at the thought of making her his mistress. Especially now he had the perfect princess tucked away in the background.

'So stop aiming for the stars and get some rest,' she commanded, and eventually sleep hit her like a mallet.

She woke with a dry mouth and a slight headache, and muscles so stiff she realised she hadn't moved all night. Groaning, she staggered out of bed and pushed the shutters open, smiling at the fresh scent of pines and the sun leaping above the sea. A small fishing boat, its bow painted with a colourful eye, puttered around the headland and across the bay.

Hastily she scrabbled into clothes and snatched her camera, running down onto the beach to catch the exquisite light. She'd never come back here, and she wanted to imprint every moment onto her heart.

An hour later, sandy and satisfied, she returned to the villa. She'd photographed sand and sea, the gorgeous little Grecian temple above the beach, the pine forest surrounding the villa, and the view from the headland.

Now, before she showered, she asked Carlotta, the housekeeper, if she could contact Lucia Bagaton.

Although the older woman appeared to speak reasonably good, if heavily accented English, Alexa must have made a mistake, for an hour later it wasn't the distant cousin of Luka who arrived at the villa, but the man himself.

'Oh! I didn't—' Alexa stopped, bushwhacked by his smile. Leashing the response fizzing through her blood, she said brightly, 'I'm sorry—I must have got it wrong. I wanted to go sightseeing, so I asked Carlotta if she could contact Lucia to arrange it. I didn't mean to drag you away from your duties.'

'I have no duties until much later in the day,' he said, smiling at the startled look on her face.

Anticipation danced through her. 'Are you bunking off?' she asked in a conspiratorial tone.

He grinned, and she noticed that he wore clothes as casual and suitable for sightseeing as hers. 'I don't spend every hour of every day ruling,' he said. 'Where would you like to go?'

It was like being given a gift from the gods. 'Your cousin Lucia mentioned something about Greek and Roman ruins,' Alexa suggested on a hopeful note, adding demurely, 'I think she felt that lovely pre-Romanesque church was a bit *nouveau* to deserve all the admiration I was giving it.' She laughed. 'And New Zealand is such a very young country that I'd like to see the oldest things you've got!'

Later, when the day was over, she thought dreamily that it had been almost perfect. Luka had shown her a Roman archway before driving up into the hills where they'd picnicked by a small jewel of a Greek temple. They'd talked as though they had known each other all their lives, almost ignoring the wildly disturbing current of attraction that ran beneath every word and glance.

Alexa had exclaimed over herbs and cyclamens growing wild, and Luka had taken her even further into the olive-silver hills to a cave where the original inhabitants of the island had sheltered. A wall, probably almost as old as the cave, enclosed the entrance.

'How long ago?' she asked, eyeing the huge blocks of stone.

He shrugged. 'Perhaps thirty thousand years.'

Awed, she said, 'That is old.'

'The oldest man-made thing on the island.' He looked at his watch. 'I'd better get you home,' he said. 'I have a meeting in half an hour.'

Until then they hadn't seen anything larger than a village, but on the way back to the villa he took her through a bustling, thriving city still full of tourists.

She leaned forward as they drove past a large building on the edge of the harbour. 'That looks ancient too,' she commented.

'A Renaissance castle built on Roman foundations,' he told her briefly.

Chilled by its size and pomp, Alexa said, 'Judging by the sentries, it must be where you live.'

'It's the official residence,' he told her coolly. 'I spend most of my time in a much smaller, more comfortable house a few miles out of town.'

She fell silent. All day she'd managed to almost forget that he ruled the country, but that big palace dominating the city reminded her of the distance between them.

He took her to the front door of the villa and said, 'I'll see you this evening.'

She gave him a pale smile. 'Thank you for a perfect day,' she said quietly.

She went slowly up the stairs and showered, and then she waited for Luka. Oh, she didn't admit that that was what she'd done during the sleepy, hot afternoon, but now, as he came out onto the terrace this evening, something slotted into place deep inside her, and she knew.

No matter what happened, she would spend the rest of her life waiting for Luka, because she loved him. Like her grandmother, she had fallen in love with a man she could never have. At least her grandmother had been loved in return, even if only fleetingly. But she wasn't going to think of that now.

Making no attempt to hide her smile, she got up and went towards him, her long skirt floating mistily around her legs.

'Hello,' she said. 'How was your meeting?' And she held out her hand.

He paused, looking into her eyes. She knew what he saw there—surrender. His lashes drooped too late to hide the swift glitter of gold as he took her fingers and lifted them to his mouth. 'Too long,' he said against her skin.

She shivered. 'Yes,' she whispered unevenly.

But after that light kiss he let her hand go and stepped back. A subtle rejection, she thought wearily, but a rejection nevertheless.

Accepting it, she forced another smile and moved away, looking over her shoulder to say, 'I'm glad you could take today off. It was glorious.'

Luka watched with half-closed eyes the sinfully distracting curve of her throat and cheek, the smooth swell of her high breasts above the narrow, lithe waist. Copper hair swung around her lovely face, and her walk was a silent, sensuous invitation that targeted his libido with unerring aim.

'I don't spend all my life on official occasions,' he said, following her.

He wasn't going to accept that invitation, even though his body throbbed with hunger for everything he knew she could give him. This time he would show her that he could be relied on to control himself.

Alexa glanced at him as she walked across to the balustrade of the terrace. His face was closed against her, the stark, uncompromising angles and lines set in a mask of forceful self-sufficiency.

It was no use telling herself that no human being could be as controlled and assured as Luka—in spite of his physical awareness of her, he'd never shown a hint of vulnerability.

Whereas she was raw with it, her love naked and exposed. Loving him was as natural to her as breathing, as necessary as her blood.

Holding desperately to her smile, she said, 'So my half-uncle and his wife arrive tomorrow. Are they staying here?'

'If that's all right with you.'

'Of course it is,' she said automatically.

'He's suggested they stay for three days.'

'Just long enough,' she said flippantly. 'If we hate each other on sight we can politely pretend otherwise for three days.' After that she'd be heading home. Her open airline ticket could be activated any time.

'You won't hate each other,' Luka said with cool confidence.

Hoping he was right, she asked impulsively, 'What's he like? I mean, I know he's a techie billionaire, and of course I know the romantic story of his escape to Australia, but what's he like as a human being?'

'Formidable,' Luka said instantly, 'but a good man.'

The word *formidable* so exactly described the man who'd just used it that she half laughed. 'Takes one to know one.'

'You'll like him,' Luka told her drily.

'I hope so.' Alexa stared down through a feathery screen of foliage to the white sand below, prisoner of the driving, irresistible awareness that had pulsed just beneath the surface during the whole wonderful day.

She said abruptly, 'This is a very beautiful place.'

'As beautiful as New Zealand?'

Suspecting him of sarcasm, she said, 'Every bit as beautiful in a different way. It looked lovely coming in from the air. I'd thought it would be dry and harsh, so I was surprised at the forests.'

'My father was passionate about forestry,' Luka said evenly.

Alexa looked around. 'And this is an enchanting spot.'

'It was my mother's refuge,' he told her. 'Her favourite cell, she used to call it.' And in an abrupt and unsubtle change of subject he said, 'I thought we'd eat down on the beach.'

'Yes, of course.'

Side by side, yet never touching, they walked through the gardens towards the little temple, shimmering in the last rays of the sun.

Carlotta had set the table in front of the columns but instead of the silver and crystal formality of the previous night she'd used rustic china and glasses. Two tall wrought-iron candelabra held candles, and food steamed in bright earthenware casseroles on a serving wagon. The earthy sophistication of the bowls and dishes somehow suited the setting perfectly.

'I know this is going to sound incredibly ignorant,' Alexa said cheerfully, 'but compared to that lovely little temple in the hills, this one looks to be in too good repair to be original.'

Luka smiled down at her. 'You've got a good eye. It's an exact replica, but it lacks soul. A hundred and fifty years ago a romantic forebear decided that it would be appropriate to build a shrine to Eros.'

The youthful god of love, Venus's mischievous son. 'It's a charming little folly,' Alexa said, skin prickling at the dismissive note in his voice.

She accepted a glass of white wine and asked him about the history of Dacia. He gave a précis of a bleak and often bloody story, but, although she found it fascinating, she preferred the edgy intimacy of their previous exchanges.

This Luka was the monarch, compelling, decisive—formidable!—master of his life. And, although she respected and admired this Luka, she had come to love the man she'd crossed swords with in exhilarating bouts, the man who'd made love with heart-stopping skill, setting a benchmark she knew no other lover would reach.

Accept it, she told herself silently, watching him through lowered lashes. Somehow, impossibly, you've fallen in love with him, and nothing is ever going to be the same again.

Alexa knew then what she was going to do before the night was through.

CHAPTER ELEVEN

ALERT as a fencer about to fight the duel of her life, she lifted her glass to hide her expression, then set it down without drinking. Delicious though the wine was, she didn't want a clouded head. Tonight she was going to experience everything, remember everything.

And so would Luka—but would he remember her as a sexual trophy, or as someone he could have loved if only his parents, forced into an unbearable situation, hadn't shattered his trust for ever?

'Are those speakers I can see?' she asked casually, nodding at the interior of the temple.

'Would you like some music?' he said, equally casual.

'I think I would,' she said slowly, adding on an unforced, husky note, 'Something good to dance to.' It was a direct challenge.

His long, measuring survey sent sensation shivering the length of her spine. Her breath hissed through her parted lips as he strode between the pillars into the dim interior. Insistent, reckless, desire drummed through Alexa.

Something about his movements reminded her of a hunter, powerful and predatory, the ruthless master of all he could see.

A moment later smooth, seductive jazz filtered through the warm air. Music to dance to? Music to make love by...

Skin prickling, she crossed to the edge of the terrace and looked out over the darkening sea.

'Alexa.'

Silently, eyes lowered, she turned. But he wasn't letting her get away with passive acceptance. A lean finger tipped her chin and he scanned her face.

Neither spoke. Alexa met his hard eyes gravely until, with a mocking smile, Luka took her in his arms. Without speaking, barely touching, they began to dance. He moved to the music with a lithe authority that overwhelmed everything but a feverish response to his lethal grace.

Bonelessly yielding to her body's urgent clamour and the violent intensity of her emotions, she melted against him. His arm tightened around her and his cheek came down on the top of her head.

'Do you like this music?' he asked into the fragrant air, a raw note rasping through the words.

'Love it,' she murmured.

Love dancing with you, her heart whispered, love everything about tonight, love you...

The heavy perfume of some unknown flower, the slight grittines of the stone terrace beneath her feet, the moody, sexy wail of the saxophone—all were integrated into the primal delight of dancing with Luka.

'So we have something in common,' he said in a cryptic voice.

Stay cool, she told herself. Striving for an easy sophistication, she said, 'We might have lots in common. We've just never bothered to find out.'

His chest lifted on a low laugh that was almost a purr. 'Too busy fighting.'

'Mmm. Instant enemies.'

'Do you know why?'

A relaxed, sophisticated woman would be lightly amused. Alexa tried for it. 'Well, there was the incident with the camera, and then the minor matter of a couple of days in a cell—'

'Before that,' he said, his beautiful mouth curving. 'Right at the start it was fireworks—skyrockets, Catherine wheels—the whole foolish, potent, mesmerising bag of tricks.'

His arm tightened a little more, pulling her closer, but when he spoke his voice was cool and reflective. 'What happened about the men who planned to attack you?'

'They were caught later that night—they attacked a woman a few streets away, but a security camera got their car number. I didn't have to give evidence,' Alexa told him, every nerve singing as he turned them both to avoid one of the white pillars, and in doing so held her for an unhurried moment against the lean strength of his body. His arms around her, the heat of his body and his subtle scent—entirely Luka and all male—overwhelmed her.

He looked at her, his autocratic face hardening in a smile of masterly irony. 'You were so inconvenient.'

'So were you! And arrogant—'

'I did overreact,' he admitted drily, pivoting again and carrying her with him. 'But I couldn't risk letting you stay free.'

Alexa nodded. 'I know.'

'I shouldn't have kissed you, or made love to you.'

A salty breeze from the sea caressed Alex's bare arms, chilling her. 'So why did you?' she asked tautly. 'I wondered if it was the old chauvinist power trip.'

His smile was unsettling with irony. 'Far from it. I simply couldn't stop myself, even though a cynical part of my brain wondered if you were prepared to barter sex for information. You slashed me with those incredible eyes, cutting as diamonds, and I wanted you more than I'd ever wanted anything else.'

Heat began to surge through Alexa in a heavy subliminal tide, drowning logic, drowning common sense.

Luka said, 'And although you were furious, you responded to me.'

Alexa stiffened and lifted her chin.

'My father discovered that the first woman I fell in love with was negotiating with one of the newspapers,' he said coolly. 'She was older than I, and had no taste for royal life; to her, it was only sensible to make what profit she could of the experience. When I broke off the affair she sold her story for a huge amount of money. I was young and foolish, but it reinforced my father's teaching that no woman can be trusted.'

'Your father was wrong,' Alexa stated.

'Intellectually I knew that. Emotionally, I still believed him.'

Quickly, to hide just how miserable that made her feel, she said, 'When I read about the peace pact I forgave you for everything. Almost—'

Laughing, he caught her fist an inch away from his ribs. 'Tigress.' With her hand wrapped in his big warm one, he bent his head and kissed her.

Yet although it began with a swift flare of passion, Alexa felt the moment his will-power slammed the gates closed in her face. Her lashes flew up as he lifted his head. Mouth clamped into a straight line, he was watching her with blazing eyes.

Driven by a fierce mixture of anger and desire and pain, she thought, Tonight he's going to lose that regal self-control.

She swayed against him, stormy hunger heating her body from the inside out. His involuntary response, a lash of darkly potent energy, swept away her last scruple.

'Luka,' she said, reaching up to run her finger across his top lip. He had shaved very recently but she felt a slight abrasion against her sensitive fingertip, a sensation that sizzled the length of her arm to explode like fire and ice in every cell of her body.

'Alexa,' he said harshly, and pulled her hand up to his mouth, biting her finger with deliberate care. And then he released her. 'I promised myself I wouldn't do this again! We need to talk.'

But she saw the hunger prowling his eyes.

'Not now,' she said, and kissed his mouth again.

He stayed rigid, asking harshly against her seeking lips, 'What do you want?'

Narrowing her eyes at him, she said, 'Can't you guess?'

He looked at her with glittering, angry intensity. 'No.' The single syllable was guttural, almost inhuman in quality.

'No, you can't guess? Or no, it's not going to happen?' She swayed into his arms again, exulting as they folded around her and clamped her against his aroused body.

Eyes dilating, Alexa saw that desperate need consume him as well, and realised the dangerous game she was playing—trying to force him into something he didn't want. A spasm of shame shattered her petty need to make him lose control.

'Neither of those. No, why fight it?' he said harshly, each word raw from his throat, and kissed her again. This time there was no holding back.

Too late she tried to let him go, but his arms tightened around her as he demanded the surrender she longed to give him. Alexa yielded, each kiss fuelling the excitement that swirled through her like rising smoke until it reached her brain and shut it down.

He tasted of love, of longing and hunger and anticipation. Ferocious pleasure cascaded through her, tearing her adrift from the world she'd always known.

When he stopped his passionate exploration she nuzzled his throat as he slid the strap of her top down her arm and followed his hand with slow, demanding kisses that liquefied her bones.

Her breath left her lungs in a moaning exclamation when he bit the smooth skin where her neck met her shoulder, gently catching her skin in strong white teeth.

Alexa knew she'd precipitated this, knew she wanted it, yet something tried to tell her that it was dangerous, terribly dangerous, and that she should pull away now while she was able to.

Except that she would die if he stopped.

Smiling blindly, helplessly, she lifted her arms and clung to him, offering herself, claiming him in the most primal and basic way of all.

She didn't resist when he picked her up. Silently she watched his face in the light of the candles while he carried her between the pillars and into the shadowed interior of the temple. Angular, stern, the handsome features revealed a self-discipline at odds with the curved fullness of his lower lip and the molten intensity of his gaze.

A sensuous rush of heat poured through her, tightening her breasts so that they thrust her nipples against the material of her top. Shuddering with delight, she accepted that if she went ahead with this she was putting her heart—her life—in the hands of a man who didn't love her.

It didn't matter. Luka wanted her and that was enough. She'd take whatever he could give, and seal this night in her heart for the rest of her life. Even if he never realised it, she'd give him the gift of her love.

As her grandmother had to her lover…

He stooped, lowering her until fine cotton cooled her hot skin, and she gazed around in astonishment. In the flickering, bobbing light of the candles through the columns she could barely discern the edges of a huge bed.

And then all coherent thought fled as Luka came down beside her. Eagerly she reached up, kissing and then licking the hollow at the base of the column of his neck where a pulse thudded rapidly.

A purring growl burst from deep in his throat. Eyes glinting like burning crystals, he thrust his hands into her hair and used the soft silk to push her head back onto the huge pillows.

Luka scanned the beautiful face raised to his, the creamy skin and the pale eyes, at once clear and blazing, as her slender fragrant body lifted against his in an involuntary invitation as old as Eve.

He could no longer resist her. Worse, he didn't want to. For the first time in his life passion fogged his brain, so that all he could think of was the hunger that devoured him, the need to bury himself deep into her and make her his own, to take everything he could from her and give in return the relentless pleasure that was already building towards a climax.

In the sensuous dimness Alexa could see nothing past the outline of his broad shoulders. Shyly she touched his face, her fingers tracing the wide cheekbones and the angular jut of his jaw, finding the contours of his mouth.

His chest expanded abruptly as he dragged in a harsh, impeded breath, and she sighed her relief into his mouth as his lips claimed hers again. When he lifted his head she was naked to the waist.

She held her breath as his mouth found her breast, and almost winced at the pleasure, keen and sharp as knives, that raced from his touch to the source of all her yearning.

'What is it?' he said against her skin, and she realised she was calling his name in a sobbing gasp. 'Alexa, tell me what you want. This…?' He moved to her other breast and the erotic torment began again.

'Or this?' he asked, the heel of one hand finding the tense, expectant place between her legs, pressing, then easing upwards in a tantalising torment.

She was ready for him, but instead of stripping her he contented himself with that tormenting imitation of the ultimate embrace until she arched into his skilful, knowledgeable, maddening hand.

'Take off my shirt,' he said.

Eyes by now accustomed to the darkness, it was a matter of moments to slide out the buttons and free him. Racked by intolerable hunger, she smoothed her hands over his shoulders and chest, delighted with the hard tensile strength of the muscles that flexed beneath her fingers.

'Yes,' he groaned.

He broke off when she slid her hand down between his trousers and his skin, her fingers delighted with the hard, hot force she found there.

Again that half-guttural, half-purring sound broke from his throat. 'Wait,' he said, and got up.

Before she had time to grieve for his absence he was back, his body as tanned and beautiful as the god for whom the temple had been built. With swift, deft movements he stripped her skirt from her and stood a moment looking down at her like a conqueror.

'I think I knew that first night,' he said, his voice harsh and dangerous, 'that this was where we'd end up.'

Words blocked her throat, refusing to be spoken. She held out her arms to him and he bent and kissed her with slow, purposeful skill until she was gasping and twisting beneath the caress of his mouth.

'Yes,' he said, that faint hint of an accent emphasised, 'now you know what it is to want as I want you...'

He positioned himself above her tense body, his long strong legs holding hers in place. She expected his previous control, but this time he thrust into her with a ferocity that almost stunned her.

It was like calling down the whirlwind. Taken over by a force beyond herself, Alexa choked out his name and moved with him, welcoming him inside her, clinging when he pulled away, winding her arms around the taut, bunched muscles of his back to hold him close to her, so that she would always remember how it felt to be his lover.

Faster and faster they moved in unison, until at last the fire swirling around Alexa tossed her into another place where sensation broke over her in merciless waves. She cried out and Luka followed her there, spilling into her as the currents of ecstasy drowned her in a sea of turbulent, erotic sensory overload.

She had no idea how long they lay there, still linked, their mutual rapture joining two people so far apart they should never have met, never have kissed, never have fallen in love.

Except, she thought, that she was the only one who loved.

But Luka had finally surrendered his formidable self-

control. At the end he had wanted her as much, as recklessly, as she wanted him.

Weakly Alexa lay against him, storing up every second, every moment, every rise and fall of his chest, the
sexy smell of their mingled sweat and lovemaking, the
gentle swish of waves on the sand and the way the candlelight bobbed between the columns.

Eventually he turned onto his side and pulled her
against him. 'When I originally came out to New
Zealand,' he said quietly, 'I was planning to marry
someone.'

A sneaking shame tarnished her indolence. No, she
thought, no, oh, no...

But it had to be faced. She would, she promised herself in one painful flash of clarity, be mature about it.
Huskily she asked, 'Are you still planning to marry her?'

'No.' He smoothed her hair back from her face, and
looked into her eyes, his own hidden beneath his lashes.
'Even after we made love on the island I thought I could
be like my father, using people for the good of Dacia.'

He pulled her into him so that she could feel his body
coming to life again. With suppressed anger he said, 'I
distrusted this violent physical attraction. At first I believed you were a modern woman, with a modern atti-
tude to lovemaking, but when I had you investigated—'

'What?' She sat bolt upright.

'I had to find out what sort of woman I was dealing
with.' A hint of arrogance brushed his voice as he pulled
her down again. 'I was delighted to find that you were
not in the habit of making love with every man you went
out with—'

'Chauvinist,' she snapped.

'—because I hoped it meant that I affected you as
strongly as you affected me.'

'How on earth did you make that out?'

He laughed and kissed the top of her head, and the throbbing little traitor in her throat. 'You made love with me the fourth time we were together,' he said outrageously.

Alexa thoughtfully sank her teeth into his shoulder. He laughed and tipped her head back, holding her in a grip that prevented movement and kept her clamped against his long, powerful body.

'My beautiful wildcat,' he said, his voice low and rough. 'I was certain that this overpowering sexual need would die when I left New Zealand, but you lodged in my mind, in my memory, like a delicious, tantalising burr beneath a saddle. After weeks of aching for you, missing you so badly that my life lost all colour and flavour, I became totally convinced that I am not like my father, able to cut my life into compartments. Fortunately I had made no overtures to my prospective bride.'

'Is she unhappy?' Alexa asked worriedly.

'No. We are very good friends, but it would have been one of those marriages of convenience you were so scornful about.'

It seemed impossible that any woman could not fall in love with Luka. Putting the princess aside for the moment, she asked, 'Why didn't you come back to New Zealand sooner?'

He paused, then said deliberately, 'I didn't know what to do. I've never felt like this before.'

'And you resented it,' she guessed.

'Resented it?' He sounded surprised.

She nodded vigorously into his chest. 'I resented it too. I was really enjoying my life and then you smashed into it, and after a while I knew nothing was ever going to be the same again. And I hate being unhappy!'

'We're a prickly pair,' he said with an odd note of laughter in his voice. 'Yes, I was angry that you could turn my life to ashes. When Alex wanted to meet you I offered my services, hoping that I would be able to look at you dispassionately as just another beautiful woman.'

'Oh, did you?' she said ominously, trying to wrench herself free of his grip.

He laughed softly and tightened his arms around her, kissing her angry, mutinous mouth with such seducing sweetness that she almost surrendered.

Luka said, 'And of course I was utterly wrong. When I saw you again I knew that you were the woman I would love until the end of my days.'

'Why didn't you say something?' she demanded, radiant with joy.

'I was sure I had made you despise me beyond recovery—and if you didn't, I thought it might be just this violence of passion, and die as swiftly as it had sprung into life, like a grass fire in summer.'

Alexa gasped as he ran an exploratory hand down her body, but before she could answer he said harshly, 'And this generous passion you give me is wonderful, but not enough. So I told you lies about Ianthe of Illyria not being able to travel so that I could persuade you to come here. And I told myself that I wouldn't make love to you.'

'I know,' she said into his shoulder. 'You posted "Keep Off" signs all around you.'

He laughed quietly. 'Being you, of course, you took no notice of them.'

Alexa's anger was fading swiftly and she couldn't help asking, 'Are you sorry?'

He kissed her. 'How can I be sorry when you can take me to heaven with one sideways glance?' He ran a hand over her back. 'When you agreed to come to Dacia I told myself that I must give you back the freedom I took from you in New Zealand. So I tried to hold aloof.' He laughed a little ironically. 'That lasted for exactly fifty-two hours.'

His grin at her sudden snort of laughter faded quickly. In a steady, almost unemotional tone he went on, 'So will you marry me, Alexa, my sweet one, my heart's delight? I love you very much, and I'm going slowly mad without you.'

She hesitated, but it had to be said. 'Even though it seems I might be related to the Illyrian Prince, I'm just an ordinary New Zealand woman—'

'I am not,' he said dangerously, 'asking you to marry me because you have some connection with Alex Considine. I would want to marry you no matter who you were. Trust is a two-way thing. Can you not trust me sufficiently to understand that you are the centre of my world, the woman I hold at my heart's core? Before I met you I was lonely, so alone and so accustomed to it that I didn't even realise it. You filled my empty heart with your vitality and your spirit and your laughter. If you won't marry me I shall never marry.'

Alexa's eyes filled with tears. 'I do trust you, and I want to marry you very much.'

'Does that mean you love me?'

'Of *course* I love you,' she spluttered. 'I think I must have fallen in love with you when Sandra Beauchamp was doing her impersonation of a piranha before that banquet!'

'I knew you wanted me,' he said in a shaken voice, holding her close. 'I hoped you'd learn to love me enough to put up with the disadvantages of living in a goldfish bowl. It seems unfair to ask you to marry me when you have no idea what you'd be getting into.'

'I don't care,' she said in a stark, stripped tone. 'I'll be with you. That's all that matters.'

But it wasn't. And those perceptive eyes saw her realisation of this. 'What is it, my darling?' he asked against her forehead. 'Whatever it is we can deal with it, I swear. If you hate the idea of living in the full glare of the media we can rapidly turn into a boring old married couple.'

Heart exulting, she said, 'It's not that.'

'Then tell me what it is.'

'Do you really trust me?' she asked quietly. 'Enough not to doubt me? I couldn't live with suspicion all the time, Luka. I love you too much. I want everything of you.'

She held her breath, but he didn't hesitate. 'I have to trust the breath in my body,' he said simply. 'I must have trusted you from the beginning. Not that I recognised it.' He paused. 'But I was certain you wouldn't go to the police with a story of abduction, and when I told you who your father was I didn't even ask myself if you would try to make money from such a story. It never occurred to me. So the trust was there, my heart, right from the start, and perhaps I should ask your pardon for ever doubting it.'

Alexa shuddered with relief. 'I'm glad,' she said inadequately.

He said soberly, 'I can't promise I'll be easy to live with, but I know in my heart and my soul that my love is safe with you, and I promise that I will take the greatest care of yours. It may take me a while to become confident enough to stop being jealous whenever you smile at another man. I can't even offer you a tranquil life. All I can promise is to love you with everything I am, everything I have, for ever.'

His stark, stripped words convinced her. She'd make him so happy he'd forget about his childhood, she vowed. Lifting her head, she looked him in the eyes.

'And I love you with everything I am,' she said unevenly, pronouncing each word like a vow. 'For ever and always, with every part of me.'

He kissed her and she melted against him.

A long time later he yawned and said lazily, 'We'll have to eat something or Carlotta will know that love has stolen all our appetites but one.'

'She knows,' Alexa said into his chest. 'Why else did she set the scene for seduction? I'll bet she thought you were being very odd last night not to stay. Mmm, you smell so good…'

'Not as good as you.' He swung off the bed and stooped to pick her up.

Alexa looked up into his beloved face. 'If you plan to jump into the water again with me,' she threatened sweetly, 'I'll do unmentionable things to you.'

A white flash in the darkness revealed his smile. 'You are a miracle,' he said quietly. 'I treated you so badly, yet you love me in spite of it. Now, if you'll put at least a layer of clothes on we can eat, and then I'll endeavour to work out how I can tactfully tell Alex Considine that he has a bride to give away.'

Three months later her half-uncle escorted her to the altar in the splendid church she'd seen from the road her first day in Dacia.

Alex Considine, Prince of Illyria, stepped back with a

smile, glancing for a moment at his now obviously pregnant wife, who smiled lovingly at him.

Clad in a silk dress the same colour as her skin, swathed in the veil that Ianthe of Illyria had worn at her wedding, Alexa looked up at the face of the man she loved.

Half an hour previously she'd panicked, but now, warmed by the special smile that was hers alone, she was totally confident. With the exquisite emerald engagement ring Luka had had made for her safely on her right hand, she held out her left and put it into his, and together they turned towards the altar and made their vows to their future.

Princes...Princesses...
London Castles...New York Mansions...
To live the life of a royal!

In 2002, Harlequin Books lets you escape to a world of royalty with these royally themed titles:

Temptation:
January 2002—*A Prince of a Guy* (#861)
February 2002—*A Noble Pursuit* (#865)

American Romance:
The Carradignes: American Royalty (Editorially linked series)
March 2002—*The Improperly Pregnant Princess* (#913)
April 2002—*The Unlawfully Wedded Princess* (#917)
May 2002—*The Simply Scandalous Princess* (#921)
November 2002—*The Inconveniently Engaged Prince* (#945)

Intrigue:
The Carradignes: A Royal Mystery (Editorially linked series)
June 2002—*The Duke's Covert Mission* (#666)

Chicago Confidential
September 2002—*Prince Under Cover* (#678)

The Crown Affair
October 2002—*Royal Target* (#682)
November 2002—*Royal Ransom* (#686)
December 2002—*Royal Pursuit* (#690)

Harlequin Romance:
June 2002—*His Majesty's Marriage* (#3703)
July 2002—*The Prince's Proposal* (#3709)

Harlequin Presents:
August 2002—*Society Weddings* (#2268)
September 2002—*The Prince's Pleasure* (#2274)

Duets:
September 2002—*Once Upon a Tiara/Henry Ever After* (#83)
October 2002—*Natalia's Story/Andrea's Story* (#85)

**Celebrate a year of royalty with
Harlequin Books!**

Available at your favorite retail outlet.

HARLEQUIN®
Makes any time special ®

Visit us at www.eHarlequin.com

HSROY02

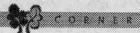

Restore the healthy balance to your life in a guilt-free way.

QUIET MOMENTS

This month, the Harlequin Presents® series offers you a chance to pamper yourself!

Enjoy a FREE Bath Spa Kit with only four proofs of purchase from September 2002 Harlequin Presents novels. Special Limited-Time Offer.

Offer expires November 29, 2002.

YES! Please send me my FREE Quiet Moments Bath Spa Kit without cost or obligation, except for shipping and handling. Enclosed are four proofs of purchase (purchase receipts) from September Harlequin Presents novels and $3.50 shipping and handling fee, in check or money order, made payable to Harlequin Enterprises Ltd.

598 KJN DNDF

Name (PLEASE PRINT)

Address   Apt. #

City   State/Prov.   Zip/Postal Code

IN U.S., mail to:
Harlequin Presents Bath Kit Offer
3010 Walden Ave.
P.O. Box 9023
Buffalo, NY 14269-9023

IN CANADA, mail to:
Harlequin Presents Bath Kit Offer
P.O. Box 608
Fort Erie, Ontario
L2A 5X3

FREE SPA KIT OFFER TERMS
To receive your free Quiet Moments Bath Spa Kit, complete the above order form. Mail it to us with four proofs of purchase (your purchase receipts). Requests must be received no later than November 29, 2002. Your Quiet Moments Bath Kit costs you only $3.50 for shipping and handling. The free Bath Spa Kit has a retail value of $16.99 U.S./$24.99 CAN. All orders subject to approval. Products in kit illustrated are for illustrative purposes only and items may vary (retail value of items always as previously indicated). **Please allow 6-8 weeks for delivery.** Offer good in Canada and the U.S. only. Offer good only while supplies last. Offer limited to one per household.

Visit us at www.eHarlequin.com   HPPOP07